ALEX MORTIMER &

THE BEAST OF
WILDEOR

D0095988

B.A.DEARSLEY

Walden House
(Books & Stuff)

For Kim

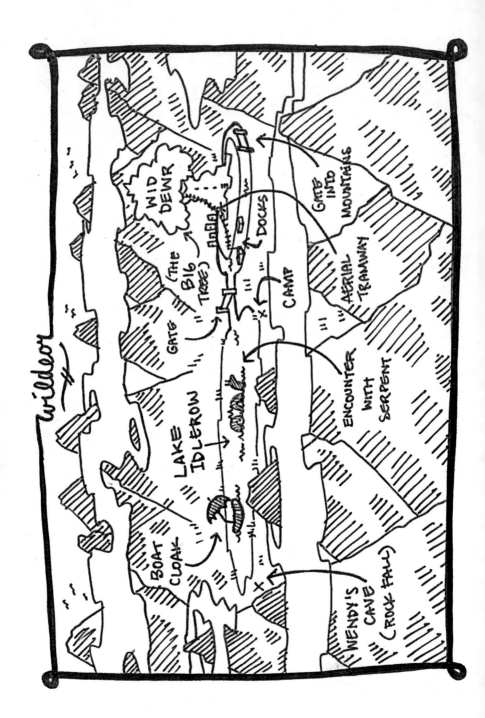

Wildeor /**wild**-door/ *n.* **1.** a secret place of sanctuary for wild beasts. **2.** a conservation area untouched by human activity. [Old English *wil* self-willed, wilful, wild; *deor* animal]

Dad was too young when he died. But during the last months of his life he managed to sort through a lifetime of clutter: childhood mementos, knickknacks from his travels, and enough paper—letters, photos, and newspaper clippings—to keep a recycling plant busy for weeks.

A few days before he passed away, he presented me with an old cigar box, dusty and damaged with age. In it was a bundle of letters. "What's so special about this stuff?" I asked curiously.

This is what he told me. His father, a captain in the British Army in the Second World War, was assigned to a secret military operation where he remained until his death in 1943. "Mom told such amazing stories about his adventures. I thought she made them up. Until I found those letters . . . and these." He handed me a dozen or so old journals.

I opened one of the musty, leather-bound books and read a few excerpts. The tidiest of handwriting stretched across the page, supplemented by numerous sketches and diagrams.

"It seems," I said, "as if whoever had kept these journals had quite the imagination."

"I thought they were stories, too. Now I'm not so sure," said Dad, stretching his frail frame out on the bed. He lay silent for a few minutes, deep in thought. "I wish I had time to figure out your grandfather's role in all of this. I want you to promise you'll find out."

I promised him I would, but events overtook us and he passed away soon after. Those letters and journals were then all but forgotten until I came across them again while sorting through some clutter of my own a few years later. Remembering the promise I'd made, I finally began reading the material he'd left me. Once started, I couldn't stop. I read of places, people, and things I'd never before heard of, although they were set in the context of familiar historical events. And as I dug deeper into the collection of journals, letters, and documents, one name kept cropping up again and again: Alex Mortimer. Some of the journals were, in fact, his. They were filled with sketches and anecdotes, a detailed record of his life as he matured from a boy to a man.

My curiosity aroused, I travelled far and wide to find out more about this untold history: across North America, Asia, Africa, and Europe. There were many dead ends, but now and then another piece of the puzzle turned up. Over time, I gained access to many incredible re-

sources related to this story: private journals, historical documents (both official and unofficial), as well as eyewitness accounts. (To protect the innocent—and, in some cases, the not-so-innocent—several names used in this book have been changed where necessary.)

The story of Alex Mortimer and the Lords of Allegiance is ready to be told—and needs to be told. As you journey on this remarkable adventure—part mystery, part prophecy—remember this: whatever your age, you have a part to play in the future of our world. You can affect change, just as Alex and his friends did. Some of you will be singled out by fate for truly special reasons (if you haven't been already!). If so, rise to the challenge. Unless you do, how will you ever know what greatness you can achieve?

And, finally, if you ever find yourself face-to-face with an enemy of the Lords of Allegiance, you better know whose side you're on!

CHAPTER 1

MAY 1915: A TRAGEDY UNFOLDS

The huge ship slipped silently through the water, a wall of cold black steel as tall and imposing as a city skyline. Waves broke harmlessly against the hull, brushed aside with barely a tremor as the ship stayed its course, homeward bound. England bound.

That such a mass of metal could move so effortlessly upon the unfriendly Atlantic never ceased to amaze Captain William Turner as he made his way to his bridge. Cunard Steamship's most respected officer, Captain Turner had crossed the Atlantic countless times. And each time he sailed aboard the miracle of machinery that was the *RMS Lusitania*, the grandest vessel of its day, he felt as safe as houses.

But this trip was different, and he'd been on edge since departing New York six days earlier. As the fighting in Europe escalated—the Great War, as it had come to be known, was almost a year old—he'd grown increasingly worried about the dangers posed to trans-Atlantic shipping. It didn't help that the *Lusitania* was carrying supplies vital to England's war effort, and was a tempting target for German submarines. Worse still, six of the ship's twenty-five huge boilers were shut down due to coal shortages, resulting in speeds well below its maximum of twenty-eight knots.

The addition of some last-minute passengers and cargo was also cause for concern. It wasn't so much the passengers that troubled him; they were a mother, her two young children, and their matronly nanny travelling under the name Ligeantia. No, it was the cargo: a sturdy metal container the size of a yacht, which bore no clues as to its contents. He'd been instructed not to record it in the ship's official manifest. Adding further to the mystery were the three men sent to guard the shipment, and the second, sealed manifest that he was told would be collected upon arrival in England.

That was all behind him now, and his attention since leaving New York had been focused on the safety of the nearly two thousand passengers and crew aboard the *Lusitania*. Upon entering the bridge, he was handed a message from Admiralty: SUBMARINE FIVE MILES SOUTH OF CAPE CLEAR, PROCEEDING WEST WHEN SIGHTED AT 10 A.M. PROCEED THROUGH CELTIC SEA.

Relieved, Captain Turner pocketed the message. "We've probably already passed it. This should calm the passengers."

The closer they got to Europe the more anxious the passengers became. The fact that the Imperial German Embassy in New York placed newspaper ads warning passengers not to travel on the *Lusitania* due to the risk of submarine attack didn't help. Nor did the rumours circulating that the three men watching over the cargo were spies sent to sabotage the ship.

As he pondered these events, a shout of "land ahoy" had Captain Turner reaching for his binoculars. He could just make out the Old Head of Kinsale, a long peninsula on the southeastern tip of Ireland, famous amongst sailors for its distinctive lighthouse with its zebra-like stripes.

"Strike a course south by southeast, steady," he ordered the helmsman. He then called for one of his junior officers: "Mr. Bestic!"

"Sir?"

"Get a fix on our position, and plot a course to Queenstown. It'll be safer than Liverpool. Hop to it! We need those bearings to get us home safely."

Confident they'd passed the U-boat threat, Captain Turner's orders changed the ship's course toward the deeper and, he believed, enemy-free Irish Channel.

* * * * *

"Your orders, sir?"

Captain Walther Schwieger, eyes glued to his periscope, cap tilted sideways so as not to obstruct his view, said nothing.

"Captain?" insisted his quartermaster, Charles Voegele. "Awaiting orders."

"Be patient. I'm thinking."

In the months they'd sailed together aboard U-20 the crew had never known their captain to hesitate. The previous two days saw them sink two English freighters, and the characteristic calm he displayed was, as always, an inspiration. But ever since he'd spotted the great ocean liner, Captain Schwieger seemed unsure of himself.

"Lanz, check that book of yours. Four funnels, schooner rig, twenty thousand tons."

The U-boat's pilot quickly found what he was looking for in his copy of *Jane's Fighting Ships*, a pre-war reference guide to the world's warships. "The *Lusitania* or the *Mauretania*, sir. Both are used to carry troops."

Captain Schwieger stepped back from the periscope just long enough to rub his aching eyes. "Those English make it too easy for you, Lanz." Although the English ship was travelling at an unusually slow speed, Schwieger knew it was out of firing range—which is exactly how he wanted things to stay.

Voegele moved closer so the other men wouldn't hear. "Sir—what's going on?"

Captain Schwieger pulled a telegram from his pocket and handed it to his quartermaster. "It came through a few hours ago. From the top."

The message read: INTERCEPT LUSITANIA. IMPERATIVE IT DOES NOT REACH ENGLAND.

"But the people on that ship have nothing to do with this damn war!" Voegele said. "A lot of them are neutrals, too."

"It's an order."

"Can't we say we didn't receive it?"

Looking at the crew crowded into the confined space of the bridge, watching intently as they awaited his next move, Captain Schwieger hesitated only briefly before turning his attention back to the periscope. "Let's hope it doesn't come to that."

Then, the unthinkable happened: the ocean liner turned away from the shelter of the coast and headed toward U-20. "What are those idiots doing? Lanz, if we fired one torpedo, how long would it take her to sink?"

"Could take hours, sir. A ship like that might never sink."

"What are you thinking?" asked Voegele.

"One torpedo might cripple her so she has to put ashore in Ireland. My orders say she mustn't reach England. Lanz, how many lifeboats does she have?"

"Forty-eight. Enough for everyone on board."

"All hands, battle stations! Load tubes one and two. Prepare to fire when ordered! Enemy speed: twenty-two knots. Angle on the bow: ninety degrees starboard. Set torpedo one to thirty knots, range seven hundred yards."

Reluctantly, Voegele relayed the command. "Tubes ready, Captain."

"Good. Flood tubes, open bow caps."

"Bow caps open, tubes flooded."

"Here it comes . . . steady. Fire torpedo one!"

The quartermaster didn't repeat his order.

"I said fire, Voegele! Now, damn it!"

"I can't! There are hundreds of children on that ship."

Pushing Voegele aside, Captain Schwieger shouted his order to the torpedo room. "Fire! Now!" The U-boat trembled as a blast of air forced the weapon out of its tube.

"Torpedo one launched, Captain!"

* * * * *

Captain Turner was leaning against the rail watching the passengers below when he heard the shout.

"Torpedo! Starboard side!"

The explosion sounded like a massive steel door being slammed shut. Seconds later, an even larger explosion rocked the ship, sending a huge column of water and debris shooting skyward like a giant fountain, demolishing parts of the upper deck and some of the lifeboats.

"Hard a-port! Get us to shore!" Captain Turner shouted to the bridge.

"She's not responding," replied the helmsman as he struggled desperately with the wheel. "And sir, all engines are out of commission."

Captain Turner's heart sank. Without power or the ability to steer, all hope for the ship was lost. "Lower the lifeboats and give the order to abandon ship. But don't launch until we've slowed enough to get everyone off."

Looking back along the port deck, Captain Turner could see that many of the lifeboats had swung inward as the ship listed and were now impossible to launch. He realized the lifeboats on the starboard side would have swung outwards and would also be out of action. Making matters worse, the passengers were beginning to panic as they made their way above deck, dazed and confused.

As the tragedy unfolded, he was distracted by the sight of a young woman trying to gain access to the stairway leading to the bridge, her path blocked by a ship's officer. In her arms was a small child no more than a few months old. "I must see the captain!" she demanded.

The officer, now recognizable to Captain Turner as Junior Officer Albert Bestic, stood his ground. "There's no time for that, madam. Make your way to the lifeboats."

"Tell him the Ligeantia must see him. He'll understand!"

Struck by the woman's calm as all around her slipped toward chaos, Captain Turner ordered Bestic to let her pass. Clutching the infant tightly in her arms, her dark hair framed a face that showed a clear sense of purpose.

"Captain, I'm sorry. We shouldn't have come."

"What do you need?"

"My son," she said, looking down at the child asleep in her arms. "I can't tell you how important he is. To all of us."

"Bestic! Place these two on the first lifeboat you find. And stay with them."

As Bestic took the young woman's arm, she stepped back, a determined look on her face. "No, I've got to find my daughter. I left her below and fear the worst." Placing the child in Bestic's arms, she turned to the captain, a pleading look in her eyes. "See that he gets to England. In case . . . I don't make it."

"Can you tell us his name?" asked Captain Turner.

Kissing the child gently on the forehead, she looked directly at the captain, as if gauging his trustworthiness. "His name's Alex. Alex Mortimer. But you mustn't tell anyone. There are those who want to harm him. I must go, I have to find my daughter—" The young woman turned and forced her way down the stairway, pushing against the passengers who were swarming the upper decks, seeking escape.

"Do as she says, man!" said Captain Turner. "And don't let the boy out of your sight."

"What about you?" asked Bestic.

"A captain belongs on his bridge. Now away with you! And God be with you!"

Captain Turner remained on deck long enough to watch Bestic, with the child clutched tightly in his arms, climb aboard one of the few lifeboats not yet launched or damaged. He breathed a sigh of relief as the junior officer took charge of the crew manning the falls, the ropes used to lower the small vessel. He'd seen too many lifeboats overturn, their passengers spilled helplessly into the water like so many rag dolls.

Leaning over the railing, he watched as Bestic's boat safely reached sea level and pulled away from the sinking ship.

Only ten minutes had passed since the first explosion, yet during this time the *Lusitania* had taken on so much water the upper decks were now almost at sea level. In the empty bridge, the water lapped at

Captain Turner's feet as he reached into his pocket for the key to his safe. Opening it, he snatched the unofficial manifest and tucked it into his waistcoat before taking hold of the wheel, bracing himself for the inevitable. As the ship slid into the icy sea, the glass doors collapsed under the pressure of the water pressing against them, sweeping Captain Turner out of the bridge.

When he regained consciousness, he found himself floating on wreckage a short distance from the sinking ship. The sea around him was a mass of death and destruction, bodies and survivors alike scattered as far as the eye could see. All that remained of the *Lusitania* was the slowly sinking stern of the once mighty ship jutting out of the water as it descended to its watery grave.

He then witnessed something that would haunt him for years afterwards. Barely visible below the water's surface, halfway between him and the sinking ship, was the dark shadow of a large sea creature heading directly towards him. At first he thought it was a whale, caught up in the terrible excitement of the *Lusitania*'s sinking. But this was unlike anything he'd ever seen before. At the last minute the creature disappeared into the depths, its wake forcing him to cling tightly to the wreckage keeping him afloat. Then, darkness.

* * * * *

In horror, Captain Schwieger watched the carnage he'd unleashed upon the *Lusitania*. "My God! We must have hit explosives. No ship should sink so easily!"

He saw only a handful of lifeboats, which meant many passengers were either dead or dying, although he could see a few survivors clinging desperately to the debris.

"Lanz! How long since we launched the torpedo?"

"Only eighteen minutes, Captain."

"We fired only one torpedo! Why two explosions?"

Scanning the horizon, he caught a brief glimpse of a large black object speeding toward the U-boat. The vessel lurched from side to side from the force of the impact. Then he heard the sound of something scraping along the hull of the submarine, accompanied by a loud, unearthly bellow like the metallic rattling of countless heavy anchor chains.

As the submarine stopped rocking, Captain Schwieger slumped to the floor, head in hands.

Lanz knelt down beside him. "What was it, Captain?"

"I don't know. It was swimming away from the *Lusitania*! Maybe a whale or something, but it was so . . . so primitive."

As calmly as he could, Captain Schwieger took up his position at the periscope, turning it in wide arcs as he searched for a sign of the monster. Seeing nothing, he lowered the periscope and gave the order the crew had been longing to hear.

"Set a course for home, Lanz. Get us out of here. Rescue ships will arrive soon looking for survivors. And us."

CHAPTER 2

SUMMER 1929: A HEAD FULL OF STEAM

The ship's stoker leant back on the old crate he used as a makeshift stool. A look of satisfaction spread across his weathered, ginger-grey-bearded face. "Put your back into it, lad. If we can't keep her at full steam we'll be late!"

"Aye aye, skipper!" replied the boy as he threw a shovelful of coal into the steamship's blazing furnace. Even though the job was dirty, Alex Mortimer didn't mind working in the boiler room of the *RMS Segwun*. He'd grown accustomed to the smell of soot, oil and engines, and enjoyed the volcano-like burst of flames as each fresh load of the heavy black fuel hit the fire.

"Less of your lip!" said the stoker, his Scots accent as broad as his shoulders. "Unless you're itchin' for a stitchin', that is."

Alex knew Red McPhee's behaviour wasn't out of character considering the time of year. As soon as the big city schools closed for the summer, the luckiest students—travelling from places like New York, Pittsburgh and Toronto—headed north to their summer homes in Muskoka. This area of rugged natural beauty, with its countless granite islands and pine-covered shorelines, had become a summer playground for the rich and famous. But for Alex and those who lived there year round, it was anything but fun—the harsh winters were long and hard. And when better weather did arrive, most of the locals, Alex included, had little time to themselves as they scratched out a living pandering to their wealthy visitors.

Most cottagers came by train, an adventurous few by plane or car. Sooner or later they'd converge upon a small pinprick on the map called Gravenhurst where they'd board the steamships of the Muskoka Navigation Company to complete their journey.

Every last one of them seemed to upset Red McPhee. "Bloody pests! They come up here just to make my life miserable," he grumbled as he wrapped his huge, black-as-coal hands around a mug of tea. "It's hard enough putting up with you all summer, Mortimer. But those toffs . . . pah! Can't stand them!"

Alex paid little attention to the barrage of complaints. It had been the same the past few years. Once the lake ice had melted, his loathsome guardian, Mrs. Pudsley, would drag him to the steamship company's offices and demand he be put to work. It was bad enough that she'd insist he toil in the boiler room—"out of sight of the better classes," she'd say contemptuously. But for Alex, the real hardship was the perverse pleasure Mrs. Pudsley seemed to get by preventing him from ever having any fun.

Despite the stoker's gruff demeanour—the locals called him "old rough as guts"—Alex didn't mind his company. Rumour had it that his reclusive, grumpy nature was the result of his being the sole survivor of a horrific explosion that decimated a munitions ship in England during the Great War. The catastrophe caused severe burns across much of his body and parts of his face, hence his tendency to hide out in the boiler room. But Alex knew Red McPhee was a big softy at heart, as evidenced by his numerous pets, some of the smallest of which (like his white mice) he'd smuggle aboard in his pockets or in his lunch pail. He was also an accomplished piper, and travellers aboard the vessel would often marvel at the deep drone of bagpipes drifting up from below deck.

Alex particularly enjoyed teasing the big man about his lack of a proper first name. Although Alex's only schooling was the knowledge he gleaned from a dusty set of nineteenth century *Encyclopedia Britan-*

nica, he was an avid reader and note taker and would write out the most unusual names he found. Then, between shovel loads of coal, he would test the big man's patience with a few new ones.

Tcchhkk! went the shovel as he thrust it into the coal pile.

"Tiberius?"

Schwooompf! went the coal as it hit the flames.

Tcchhkk!

"Thelonius?"

Schwooompf!

Tcchhkk!

"Adonis?"

Schwooompf!

Tcchhkk!

"Algeo, that's a good one!"

Schwooompf!

Red McPhee sighed deeply. "Isn't there someplace else you'd rather be, Mortimer? Somewhere someone actually wants you?"

Ignoring the snide remark, Alex gave the stoker a mock salute. "To the former Red McPhee, I hereby bestow the name of . . . ahem . . . Sasquatch!"

Red McPhee, Sasquatch

"That does it, you silly bu—"

Alex ducked as the stoker flung a lump of coal at him, barely missing him as he dodged out the way.

"You're aimin' for a maimin', aren't you lad? What kind of daft

11

name is that?"

"It's all over the front pages! There've been tons of sightings around the Rockies of some huge ape-man. A lot of other strange animals, too. But I thought this hairy Sasquatch thing sounded a bit . . . well, like you."

This time, the coal Red McPhee flung hit Alex where it hurt most. "Owwww, jeesh! I was just kidding!"

"Well, unless you're cruisin' for another bruisin', get cracking with that coal, laddie."

Despite the taunts, Alex knew Red McPhee liked him. Sure, he was a somewhat cocky assistant, but he was strong for his age and felt comfortable around machinery.

While his face was not yet what you'd call handsome, it held promise. Though not quite man enough for a moustache, Alex had a faint trace of dark hair—"bum fluff", Red McPhee taunted—on his upper lip. Another sign of his entry into the turbulent years of adolescence was the occasional appearance of that ancient enemy of teenagers, *acne vulgaris* (a Latin term for 'spot' that Alex had included on a previous list of alternative names for Red McPhee).

His dark hair was styled in typical late 1920s fashion: slicked back tightly across the scalp, smooth and shiny, held firmly in place with a generous helping of Murray's Superior Pomade, one of the few indulgences Mrs. Pudsley permitted.

"You're a good worker," said Red McPhee, throwing a rare compliment Alex's way. "Even if you are a right pain in the arse sometimes."

The ship shook with the shrill blast of its whistle. Startled by the sudden noise, Red McPhee leapt off his crate, spilling tea over himself in the process. "Blast Captain Larson and his bloody whistle. Gets me every time!" Grabbing an oily rag, he dabbed at the stain now mingling with countless others on his dirty overalls. "My best frock, too!"

Tossing the dirty rag at Alex, Red McPhee grabbed the nearest shovel and made as if to swat him with it. "You best be on your way, we'll be docking soon. And clean yourself up before that nasty old Pudsley woman sees you. Go on, away with you."

Wiping his coal-covered hands on his dirty overalls, Alex pocketed the rag and climbed the short ladder to the doorway leading out of the stuffy, dark boiler room. As he reached the top rung, a shadow fell across the narrow opening. Squinting into the daylight, his heart skipped a beat when he saw the silhouette of Sarah Greystone, one of the few cottagers he recognized. Like Alex, Sarah was fourteen, but that was where the similarities ended. Whereas Alex was forced to work hard and knew few comforts, Sarah's existence was one of unbridled privilege: what Sarah wanted, Sarah got (or so Alex had been told by Mrs. Pudsley). The only child of world-renowned archeologists, she was a clean freak, as concerned about appearances as Alex wasn't.

As she glanced down at him on her way through the ship, Alex hesitated, conscious of the tremendous social divide between them. Horrified, he watched as she stopped, a wide smile spreading across her pretty face. To his surprise, she leant forward and extended a perfumed hand—she smelt clean, he thought, like soap and flowers.

"You're Mrs. Pudsley's boy, aren't you?" she said boldly. "Alex, isn't it? I'm Sarah. I didn't know you worked the steamers."

Alex hesitated, unsure whether Sarah wanted to shake his hand or help him up the ladder.

"Well?" she said impatiently. "I don't have all day."

Alex held out his hand, impressed at her grip as she helped him out of the boiler room. "I see you around all the time in the summer with your mother."

"She's not my mother," Alex blurted out a little too strongly. "I mean, sorry, it's just . . . never mind."

Although he'd often seen Sarah with her family—her cottage and his home shared the same laneway—Alex had never before spoken to her: which is why, scruffy as a chimney sweep, he found himself at a complete loss for words as he gazed upon the vision before him. Her tidy summer outfit of walking pumps, white slacks, and close-fitting, blue-striped blouse seemed to shimmer in the sunlight. Her long, vibrant, red hair was tucked up under a large floppy-brimmed hat worn to keep the sun off her fair skin.

Unlike Alex, Sarah did stand out in a crowd. Although she'd never admit it, that was the desired effect. Tall for her age, she was slender and carried herself with an air of confidence that most people mistook for an aloofness born of her privileged upbringing in New York.

"Are you getting off at Mortimer's Point?" she asked. "Perhaps you could walk me to the cottage? My parents aren't there yet, and I could use some help with my luggage."

"Sure," replied Alex, hoping he didn't sound too eager.

"Your mother, I mean, Mrs. Pudsley, is going to help out until my parents arrive. Maybe we could go boating or something?"

Before Alex could respond, he felt a firm hand on his shoulder. He turned to see the ship's captain scowling at him. "Caught you, Mortimer! You shouldn't be up here bothering the passengers. State you're in, I ought to throw you overboard! That'd clean him up, wouldn't it, Miss Greystone?"

Alex tried in vain to shrug off Captain Larson's strong hand. "I'm sure your passengers wouldn't let you," he said, looking to Sarah for support.

"Don't look at me. I'd probably help."

Captain Larson laughed heartily at Sarah's response. "What'll people say if they see a tramp like you waltzing about on my ship? Eh?"

To Alex's relief, the captain loosened his grip and steered him toward the ship's bow. "You can use my cabin to clean up, Mortimer. And you, young lady," he said, extending his arm in a gentlemanly fashion, "you can watch us dock from the wheelhouse. First class all the way up there!"

Once in the captain's cramped cabin, Alex removed his overalls and washed off as much grime as he could before making his way nervously to join Sarah. He found her leaning over the railing, watching the passengers below.

"Very spiffy! I hardly recognize you," she said. "By the way, did I hear the captain say you're a Mortimer?"

"Yes, why?"

"It's just . . . well, I thought I knew all the Mortimers up here. No one ever said anything about you."

Before Alex could say anything more, Captain Larson beckoned him to the wheelhouse. "Give her a blast of the whistle to let them know we're coming. It'll wake up that lazy McPhee, too."

Alex gave the steam whistle's chain a sharp tug, and the haunting sound rumbled up from the bowels of the ship and echoed across the lake. Grinning from ear to ear, he gave an extra pull just to be sure.

"Don't overdo it," said Captain Larson. Then, with a sly wink, he added: "Best go see your young lady friend."

Rejoining Sarah, Alex scanned the shoreline for a landmark. He soon spotted Seagull Island, a tiny rocky blemish on the otherwise mirror-flat surface of the lake. They were just minutes from home, and Alex wanted to savour every moment spent with his new friend—and away from Mrs. Pudsley.

The sudden noise of an aircraft engine approaching fast from the stern of the ship distracted Alex, who turned in time to see a large, brightly coloured floatplane skim over the shoreline and pass low overhead. The deep pulsing growl of its engine—all thunder and lightning, thought Alex—caused Captain Larson to duck instinctively, knocking his cap off in the process. Alex couldn't help but snicker as it tumbled into the water.

"He'll pay for that!" bellowed the captain angrily, waving his fist at the floatplane as it roared up the lake.

"Wow! Did you see that?" said Alex. "That was so fast, so—"

"Noisy!" said Sarah, lowering her hands from her ears. "The captain's right. That crazy flyboy could have caused an accident."

Sarah had to cover her ears again as the *Segwun*'s whistle signalled their approach to Mortimer's Point, the small collection of rustic cottages and ramshackle year-round dwellings that Alex called home. The ship then made a sweeping starboard turn around the last few small islands between it and the mainland before lining up gracefully for the final yards of this leg of the journey.

"Hard astern!" shouted the captain as they made their approach.

"Hard astern!" came the reply.

The ship slowly slid into its moorings, the only sound the gentle hiss of steam escaping through its smokestack and the clanging of the engine room levers as it glided to a halt.

From his vantage point adjacent the bridge of the *Segwun*, Alex had a clear view of the docks at Mortimer's Point, a regular stop for the steamships as they ferried passengers and supplies to and from the area's cottages and hotels. Sightseers in their bright summer best watched as the deckhands strained to pull the ship's thick, coarse lines tightly around the mooring bollards, securing her to shore. A little distance away, a small crowd had gathered around a floatplane with a bright orange fuselage and yellow wings, which was tied at the far end of the dock.

Exiting the bridge, Captain Larson harrumphed angrily into his beard. "That's the bandit who attacked us! Noisy bloody thing. And look at it, taking up half the dock! Who does he think he is?"

Alex watched with keen interest as the pilot emptied the contents of a gas canister into the plane's fuel tank. "Whose is it?" he asked.

"No idea. Never seen a fancy one like that up here before. Owes me a new cap, though." Captain Larson then turned his attention to the activity on the dock. "Come on, pull her in! We've got to get these people off and be on our way!"

But Alex had problems of his own.

"Mort-i-mer! I see you up there. Stop your lollygagging and get down here this minute!"

It was Mrs. Pudsley.

CHAPTER 3

DOUBLE-CHINNED AND DOUBLE-CROSSED

Mrs. Pudsley stood out like a sore thumb. Although not quite round, she was as wide as she was tall. She looked, thought Alex, like one of those wooden Russian dolls—pop off her head and a slightly smaller version would be revealed. Where her neck should have been, a large roll of flesh cascaded from her chin to her gravity-defying bosom. Bushy eyebrows underscored her ever-frowning forehead, a single straight line of hair stretching above her eyes like a large furry caterpillar.

Alex had known Mrs. Pudsley for as long as he could remember—too long, in fact. Like Alex, she was of English origin and had been the family's nanny when his parents died during the Great War. After being appointed his guardian, she had for some inexplicable reason relocated to the tranquil backwaters of Mortimer's Point, taking Alex with her.

"Looks like old pudding face is on the warpath," said Sarah.

Although Sarah's frankness surprised Alex, his stomach still churned as he watched Mrs. Pudsley wade through the crowd, her elbows nudging aside anyone who dared get in her way.

"What did you call her?"

"Pudding face. You said she wasn't your mother, and it's obvious you don't like her. She does look like one, doesn't she? I mean, see how that chin wobbles? Like pudding."

"Mort-i-mer! Mooort-eeeee-merrrr!" bellowed the housekeeper. "Get your backside down here this minute. Chop, chop!"

Mrs. Pudsley's tongue-lashing began the moment Alex stepped ashore. It was always the same. If not complaining about his appearance, she'd complain about his tardiness or disrespectful tone, though he seldom got a word in edgewise. Nothing was ever right in Mrs. Pudsley's negative little world.

"What is it with you?" she said, spitting the words as Alex stood before her. "You're nothing but t-r-u-b-e-l. Trouble!"

Alex failed to stifle a giggle at Mrs. Pudsley's mangled spelling, and tried to duck as she swatted him across the back of the head. "How dare you laugh at me!"

Sarah had by now joined them on the dock, the ship's crew having deposited a small mountain of luggage at her side.

"Ah, Miss Greystone. How nice to see you, my dear, very nice indeed."

Alex winced at the ingratiating tone his guardian adopted. It was the same one she used whenever in the presence of those she considered as being from the better classes. He was embarrassed that his new friend had to see him in the company of the brown-nosing old woman.

Mrs. Pudsley rubbed her hands together and smiled menacingly as she sidled closer to Sarah. "I promised your parents I'd keep good care of you. I assure you this will be a summer you'll never, ever forget. Either of you." Then, looking disapprovingly at Alex, she added: "Stop being such a lazy lout! Collect the young lady's belongings and follow me. We don't want to be late."

18

"Late for what?" asked Sarah.

"Just a little surprise I've arranged, my dear. Let's get a move on, shall we? I've got something to collect from the lodge. By the time I'm out, I'd like you both to be well on your way to the Greystone cottage."

With a final nod toward Sarah, Mrs. Pudsley headed in the direction of Heather Lodge, the hotel that also served as the store and Post Office at Mortimer's Point. Once out of earshot, Sarah turned to Alex, wrinkling up her nose in disgust. "She gives me the heebie-jeebies! Does she always smell that bad?"

"You mean, like vinegar and mothballs?"

"More like vinegar and old teeth!"

Alex laughed. As he turned to help with her luggage, his attention was drawn again to the floatplane that buzzed them earlier. The pilot, having finished refuelling, was looking their way. Catching Alex's attention, he waved.

"Is he waving at you, Sarah?"

"Who?"

"That aviator. He looks kind of familiar."

"Hi there!" the pilot called out as he made his way toward them. "Say, are you Alex Mortimer?"

Alex nodded.

"Then you, young lady, must be Sarah Greystone. You sure fit the description. So does your charming friend, Miss Manners over there," he said, nodding in the direction of Mrs. Pudsley. The film-star handsome pilot, his hair an unruly mess of black curls, pulled a small notebook from his flying jacket and read the following descriptions from the page: "Alex Mortimer, fourteen, dark hair, slender build, usually scruffy and covered in coal dust—although not today, it would appear. And then there's Sarah Greystone: fourteen, red hair, summer hat, immaculately dressed and mannered. As for Mrs. Pudsley—" the pilot stopped reading, placing the notebook back in his jacket. "Well, I better not repeat what was said about her. It's not at all pretty."

"Who gave you that information?" asked Sarah, flustered. "I mean, who are you?"

"The name's Donnelly. Lonnie Donnelly."

"That's it!" said Alex excitedly. "You're the guy who shot down the

Red Baron!"

"Well, I was there when it happened."

Lonnie Donnelly was, in fact, quite the celebrity. Earlier that year he'd flown desperately needed medicine through blizzards to a remote Arctic community, an epic flight in an open cockpit in subzero temperatures. The heroic deed saved lives and resulted in many young men wanting to become pilots, Alex included. And although he didn't actually shoot down the notorious German ace eleven years earlier, he was certainly there when it happened. His squadron was embroiled in a dogfight with the famous Flying Circus when his guns jammed. The Red Baron, sensing an easy kill, pounced. Fortunately for Lonnie, his squadron leader came to the rescue, firing the burst of bullets that sent the German pilot crashing to his death.

Such was the pilot's fame that Sarah, too, had read of his escapades. Which is why, after straightening her hat, she extended her hand in a ladylike manner. "Ahem." She coughed, waggling her hand to be sure he got the message. Taking Sarah's hand, the pilot placed a somewhat clumsy kiss upon it. Despite her apparent boldness, Sarah's complexion reddened until it matched her hair.

Alex, excited at meeting one of his heroes, extended his hand in friendship. "I'm pleased to meet you, too, Mr. Donnelly, sir."

"What, you want a kiss, too?"

Alex whipped his hand away quickly.

"You guys can call me Mop, most people do. The hair, you see. Can't do anything with it. Can't repeat what your captain friend called me, though. At least not in front of a lady! Made me pay for a new cap, too."

Pointing at the pilot's weathered flying jacket, Alex asked: "Is that the jacket the Red Baron shot up?"

"Sure is," said Mop, reaching around and poking his finger through a hole in the jacket's left side. "Another inch and I wouldn't be here talking to you."

"We saw you as you were landing. Scared the pants off the captain, but I thought it was fantastic! Love your airplane. What is it?"

"This little sweetheart is the Travelair 6000, the limousine of the air! A beauty, isn't she? No more open cockpits for me! No sir. Now, if you don't mind, we've got to get going."

"*We* must be going?" asked Sarah, looking around to see if the pilot had anyone else travelling with him. Seeing no one, she added: "Surely you mean you must be going?"

"No, I meant we. You, me, and Alex. We've only got a few minutes before they come for you."

Sarah looked confused. "Is this to do with my parents?"

"Kind of. It also has a lot to do with your young pal here, too. I'll tell you what I know once we get going."

"Why should I . . . why should we . . .trust you?" asked Sarah. "We don't even know you."

The pilot took a crumpled telegram from his pocket and handed it to Sarah. "It's from your parents. It came yesterday, from Ethiopia. It'll vouch for me."

Unfolding the telegram, Sarah read the contents aloud: "Lonnie. Our discovery puts everyone in danger. Important package sent to Mortimer's Point. Keep safe. Collect daughter Sarah and boy, Alex, who lives with Mrs. Pudsley. Execute escape plan immediately. Trust no one. Repeat. No one. They are on to us. Your friends, the Greystones."

Sarah, looking a little bewildered, handed the telegram back to Mop. "Are they in some sort of trouble?"

"We're all in trouble. There'll be time to talk later. But you must believe me. You're in serious danger, both of you. Let's get that luggage onboard before Mrs. Pudsley returns, and then see if we can find that package your parents sent."

As if on cue, Mrs. Pudsley exited Heather Lodge clutching a small parcel. Seeing she'd been spotted, she quickly tucked it into her purse and waddled over to determine the cause of the holdup. "Young man, you mustn't pester the children."

Mop took a step backwards as Mrs. Pudsley tried to snatch the suitcase from him. "Alex and Sarah will not be going anywhere with you!"

Taking hold of the suitcase's handle, Mrs. Pudsley tugged sharply on it. "Why, of all the nerve!" she said. "The children are in my care, so if you'd kindly let go, we'll be on our way!"

Mop held his ground. Alex had never before seen anyone stand up to the strong-willed woman. "No, you listen to me," said the pilot. "They need to get as far from you as possible. So beat it before your so-called friends get here. They don't suffer fools kindly, and you're a very foolish woman. And hand over that package."

"I don't know what you mean," said Mrs. Pudsley indignantly, still clutching the suitcase tightly.

Unnerved by the tug-of-war between Mrs. Pudsley and the pilot, Sarah tried to intervene by grabbing hold of the suitcase, too. Already close to bursting, it broke open, spilling its contents onto the dock. Alex stooped to help her gather up her belongings.

"Will someone please tell me what's going on?" said Sarah, distraught by the turn of events.

"This woman has double-crossed you," said Mop, kneeling to lend a hand. "What'd they promise you, Pudsley? Money? Jewels?"

Mrs. Pudsley, out of breath, red-faced and flustered after tangling with the pilot, did her best to feign ignorance. "How dare you! I've never heard such—such rubbish! Please leave the children alone and be on your way, and we'll pretend this—"

The loud rumble of a powerful inboard engine drowned out the rest of Mrs. Pudsley's ranting. Alex turned to see the sleek, bullet-shaped hull of a mahogany speedboat zip past the docked steamship, narrowly avoiding hitting the docks as it slowed.

Gathering as much luggage as possible, Mop motioned Alex to do likewise. "They're early. Follow me!" he shouted as he led the way to the floatplane. Throwing Sarah's suitcases into the passenger area, Mop then jumped into the cockpit. Tossing the luggage he was carrying into the plane, Alex saw two athletic blond-haired men, dressed head to toe in black, jump ashore. As the first tied up the boat, the second struggled to keep hold of two fierce dogs pulling hard against their leashes, barking madly. The crowd of onlookers quickly dispersed.

Mrs. Pudsley lunged at Alex and Sarah in an attempt to prevent them escaping into the floatplane. In her desperation, she grabbed a handful of Sarah's hair, knocking the girl's hat into the water in the process. Sarah instinctively swung her hand at the older woman, hitting her forcefully across the face. Shocked, Mrs. Pudsley let go and stepped backwards, almost tipping into the lake. Teetering on the edge of the dock, her arms flailing madly as she tried to keep her balance, she grabbed hold of the only thing close enough to prevent her from falling in—Alex.

"Pull me in, boy, quickly, or I'll . . . I'll—"

Before she could finish, she was drowned out by a deafening blast of the *Segwun*'s whistle as the ship signalled its imminent departure. At the same time, the ship's large propellers kicked into action, churning the water a few feet below the stout woman.

"Or you'll what?" asked Alex, holding Mrs. Pudsley's arms while trying to keep his balance.

Seeing his predicament, Sarah grabbed Alex around the waist. "Give me the package or we'll let you fall!" she shouted.

"Take it! It's in my purse!"

Sarah leant forward and reached into Mrs. Pudsley's purse for the package. Tucking it into her skirt, she placed her hands on Mrs. Pudsley's wrists and with a heave helped Alex pull the heavy woman upright.

Straightening her clothing after her close call, Mrs. Pudsley then tried snatching the package back from Sarah. Alex impulsively placed himself between the two women. "Why'd you do it? What'd I ever do to you?"

"It's all your fault!" she said bitterly. "I was with your mother when that ship sank. I tried to stop her, but she wouldn't listen. She went looking for your sister. Your dad blamed me. They all did."

"What do you mean?"

"Why else would I be sent here? Snow all winter, bugs all summer. I h-a-i-t hate it! They told me I only had to look after you here for a year, then they'd send me back to England. It's been fourteen years and they've forgotten all about me! Then . . . then those nice men offered me a ticket back to England, even a house of my own, if I helped them get hold of you and the girl. But . . . but they promised they wouldn't hurt you! They just had some questions, that was all."

Angered by Mrs. Pudsley's confession, Sarah shoved her backwards toward the lake. The older woman let out a cry as she lost her balance, splashing into the churning water behind the steamship's spinning propellers.

"She can't swim!" shouted Alex.

"Good! No one messes with a Greystone and gets away with it."

Grabbing a nearby life ring, Alex tossed it to Mrs. Pudsley as she floundered, cursing and swearing, behind the steamship.

The floatplane's propeller spun into life with a deep roar as Mop fired up the engine, and a snort of dark smoke shot through the exhaust. Stepping back onto the dock, Mop ushered Alex and Sarah into the cramped passenger area, slamming the door behind them. Along with the luggage, the plane held a dozen or more gas cans. As the pilot untied the floatplane, Alex saw the two men running toward him, the two fierce dogs now off their leashes.

"Mop, look out!"

Pulling what looked like a pendant from his pocket, Mop waved it in front of the approaching hounds. To Alex's astonishment, they stopped dead in their tracks and cowered on their bellies before the pilot. With a shout, Mop lunged at them, shaking the pendant. Frightened, the dogs turned and ran away as fast they could, nearly knocking over their masters in their haste.

"That showed them!" said Mop triumphantly, climbing back into the cockpit and handing Alex the pendant.

Alex could barely hide his excitement. "Whoa! That was incredible! They looked like they were going to kill you, then—then they turned chicken! How'd you do it?"

"It wasn't me. It's the amulets. No idea what's in them, but I've yet to meet an animal that didn't think twice about hurting me after seeing one." Reaching into his jacket, Mop pulled out a second amulet. "Here's one for you, too, Sarah. Keep them safe."

Alex slipped the amulet around his neck and tucked it safely into his shirt. He noticed Sarah slip hers into her pocket. "You're not going to wear it?"

"I've no need for a necklace to keep crazy animals away. Besides, it's ugly."

As the floatplane pulled away from the dock, Alex alerted Mop to the fact the two dog handlers had climbed back into their boat. No sooner had they cast off when the *Segwun* positioned itself directly between them and the floatplane, blocking their exit from the cramped harbour area. Glancing up at the ship's bridge, Alex caught a glimpse of a capless Captain Larson waving as he gave a few sharp blasts of the steam whistle.

"There's not much room for takeoff!" Mop shouted over the din of the engine as he pushed the floatplane's throttle wide open. "We're carrying way too much weight with all the extra gas and luggage. We're going to need all the lake we can get! Hang on to your hats and hope we clear those trees."

"You're kidding?" squealed Sarah.

"Nope! And I think those guys are mad at me for setting their dogs loose."

Alex saw the sleek speedboat finally squeeze past the *Segwun*, its bow rising out of the water menacingly as it picked up pace. It had little problem catching up with the floatplane as both machines raced across the lake. "Who are they?" he shouted.

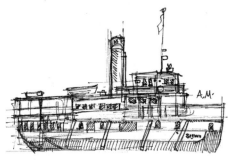

"Ultima. They're like every crook you've ever heard about all rolled into one. Only worse."

Alex felt helpless as he watched one of their pursuers climb onto the bow of the speedboat as it bucked across the lake, then leap the narrow gap between the two machines. Landing heavily on the float, he clung tightly to the aircraft, his legs skimming the water as he inched his way forward. Pulling himself upright and holding onto the wing strut, he used his free hand to pull a pistol from a holster under his shirt. "Mop! He's got a gun!"

"Nothing I can do. Sort it out yourselves!"

Before Alex could react, Sarah leapt into action, throwing open the passenger door so forcefully it knocked the gun from the stranger's

25

hand. She then swivelled in her seat and, drawing both legs up to her chest, kicked hard, sending him careening backwards into the lake, where he narrowly avoided being hit by the speedboat.

"That'll teach him to ruin my day!" she said, matter-of-factly.

"Nice work!" shouted Mop, glancing backwards. "But what about the boat? I need more time."

Without thinking, Alex grabbed a suitcase from the heap at the back of the floatplane. Dashing to the open door, he hurled it at the speedboat as it closed in to ram the floatplane. The suitcase burst open as it hit the windscreen, its contents—predominantly underwear, Alex couldn't help but notice—smothering the driver.

Moments later, the floatplane rose sharply out of the water, throwing Alex to the ground as its floats smacked loudly against the top of the tall pine trees closest to the water's edge. Alex stood up just in time to see the speedboat plow into the rocky shoreline. With a loud *whump* it exploded, sending a small mushroom cloud skyward.

"Holy cow! Exploding underwear!" he said.

"Couldn't you have thrown something else?" said Sarah angrily.

Alex shrugged apologetically.

"They must have been planning to take out Mortimer's Point with explosives once they got you guys. Always showing off. That's the last we'll see of those two, but there'll be more of them, a lot more. Now buckle up, things can still get dicey."

Sarah took a seat next to Alex and tapped Mop on the shoulder. "Where are we going?"

"A safe place a long, long way from here. There's a change of clothes back there. Hiking boots and stuff. And food. I could sure use a bite to eat after all that excitement."

Sarah reached for the nearest backpack. "I hope we never have to go through anything like that again."

Mop smiled broadly. "I promise. And I never make promises I can't keep."

CHAPTER 4

A HEAD IN THE CLOUDS

"Keep it steady, Alex. He'll fall off!"

Alex kept his eyes fixed firmly on the pilot, all the while doing his best to keep the floatplane level. "I'm trying my best. It's a lot harder than it looks!"

Mop clung to the right side of the aircraft's nose, his feet placed firmly on one of the floats, sleeves rolled up and a determined look on his face as he was buffeted by the wind blasting past him. Gripping the cowling, he used his free hand to wipe the build-up of oil from each spark plug, the cause of the floatplane's misfiring engine, before tightening them in place with a wrench. Alex watched anxiously as Mop lowered the cowling and sidled carefully back to the cockpit. Giving a thumbs up, Mop's expression changed dramatically as he appeared to lose his balance and disappeared from view.

"Did he fall?" Sarah searched frantically for a sign of the pilot, her face pressed against the glass of the passenger window.

Before Alex could even respond, the pilot popped up on the other side of the floatplane. Sarah let out a yelp of surprise. Pulling open the cockpit door and laughing, Mop plunked himself down beside Alex. "Gets 'em every time!"

A very annoyed Sarah punched him on the arm as he took over the controls. "That was stupid!" she said. "What if you really did fall off? We'd all be toast!"

"Heck, that was nothing compared to the stunts I got up to back in my barnstorming days."

Still unimpressed with Mop's shenanigans—it didn't help that Alex hadn't stopped laughing—Sarah crossed her arms and sank back into her seat. "How much longer do I have to stay up here in this crate? I'd be better off stuck down there in the middle of nowhere than up here with you two."

"Could be arranged," Mop muttered as he tapped the aircraft's fuel gauge. "We'll have to start thinking about refuelling soon."

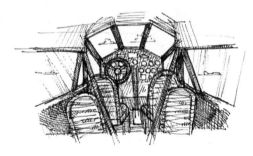

Thanks to modifications he'd made to the fuel tanks, the floatplane could fly great distances before running out of fuel. It had been nearly seven hours since their hurried departure from Mortimer's Point, now some 650 miles behind them. While Sarah spent most of that time reorganizing what was left of her luggage or hiding in the tiny washroom at the rear of the plane, Alex stayed up front, relishing every minute spent with the war ace and marvelling at the scenery far below. He'd never before fully appreciated the vastness of the wilderness that occupied so much of the continent. "It's never-ending," he said. "Not a sign of civilization anywhere."

"You can say that again," said Sarah. "Especially up here. Can't we just go home?"

"Not after what happened this morning," replied Mop. "You might just as well relax and enjoy the view. Your parents always liked the wilderness, Sarah. The wilder the better."

"What do you mean?"

Mop remained silent, as if he'd said too much.

For Alex, the day had been a blur of activity, most of it a little crazy, but all of it thrilling. After years of being stuck in the backwater that was Mortimer's Point, any adventure was a good adventure. But Sarah wanted answers.

"We're attacked by rabid dogs and lunatics with guns, you nearly get us killed in a ridiculous boat chase. Now you're taking us God knows where talking gibberish about some guys called Old Tuna or something."

"Ultima," corrected Mop.

Sarah grew increasingly agitated. "Tell us what's really going on, or you can turn this tin can around! And take us someplace people aren't trying to kill us. Preferably without trees!"

In an effort to ease the tension, Alex pointed to a glimmer of light reflecting off a large expanse of water some distance in front of them. "What lake's that?"

"That, my young friend, is called perfect timing! We'll be refuelling there."

Alex gave Mop a quizzical look. "Where do we get gas down there?"

"Not down there, up here. We're refuelling in the air!"

Sarah shook her head in disbelief. "Tell me you're kidding. You are kidding, aren't you?"

"Don't worry, I've worked everything out. So long as we don't make any mistakes, it'll be a breeze. The supply plane should be here shortly. Who's got a watch handy?"

Alex pulled his pocket watch out of his shirt pocket. "It's eleven minutes after six, exactly."

Mop nodded his thanks as he studied the ground below. "About twenty minutes or so before refuelling."

"How can you tell?"

"Air tracking. Just watch for any subtle changes in scenery. Different tree types, rock formations, streams and trails, that kind of thing. At night, it's all about the sky, and the position of the moon and the stars. If that doesn't work . . . hell, follow your nose."

Mop's attention was drawn to Alex's watch. "Nice timepiece.

Where'd you get it?"

"It was my dad's. His name's on it." Alex turned the watch over. "It says, 'Morty. One of the few. Colonel Walden.' I've no idea who Colonel Walden was, though. Must've been a friend."

"Take the controls for a minute. I'd like to see that thing. Hmmm . . . this isn't any old pocket watch," said Mop, holding the watch up admiringly by its thick gold chain. "It's a trench watch. British officers used them before wristwatches became popular. Looks older than the Great War, though . . . probably turn of the century, maybe even Boer War."

"My dad was in the British army?"

"Looks that way." Mop opened the watch case, revealing a small, grainy photograph. "Handsome couple. I guess the baby is you?"

Alex shook his head. "It's my sister. She and my mother died when I was little . . . Dad too."

Mop took a small knife from his jacket and picked at the edges of the photo. "Well, well, what have we here?"

Exposing the watch's internal mechanism, he pressed down on one of the tiny gears, causing a previously hidden compartment at the back of the watch case to open. Prying it open, delicately, he revealed an engraved W with an ornate sea serpent wound around it. Under it were the words DOMNE WILDEOR.

"Hmm . . . interesting. Do you know what it means, Alex?"

"Haven't a clue."

Closing the pocket watch, Mop handed Alex back his prized possession and took over control of the plane. "Funny. You're not at all what I expected."

"I don't think he's quite what any of us could have expected," continued Sarah. "Anyway, Mop, what's Domne Wildeor?"

"It's not so much a what as a who. Whoever Colonel Walden was, or is, he must have been a military man, too. He also knew your dad was a pretty important guy. Dominatio means lord or king in Latin. And Wildeor is a place."

Sarah continued with her line of questioning. "Domne Wildeor means Lord of Wildeor?"

"Right."

"So Alex's dad was the Lord of Wildeor, whatever that place was?"

"Not was, is."

"But his dad's dead. So does that mean Alex is the new Lord of Wildeor?"

"Afraid so," said Mop.

Sarah then turned to look at Alex. "What kind of Lord-of-anything could be so scruffy?"

Embarrassed, Alex slunk into his seat.

Mop patted Alex on the shoulder, reassuringly. "No offence, Alex, but she does have a point. No one votes for you guys. Anyway, I have a hunch there's a great deal more to you than meets the eye. Tom can tell you more about it. He's good at all this old prehistory stuff."

"Tom who?" asked Sarah.

"Tom Liat. Tom W. Liat, to be exact. Your parents introduced me to him years ago. A little eccentric, but smart. Knows everything about everybody. And old. Really old. It was Tom who gave me those amulets. He said I'd know exactly who to give them to when the time came."

Alex reached for his amulet, all but forgotten since their hasty departure from Mortimer's Point. Clasping it by its sturdy gold chain, he was struck by its beauty and craftsmanship. The size of a silver dollar, it was made of a crystal-like substance encasing a red jewel that glowed brightly as if on fire. Alex touched it delicately, almost expecting it to burn him.

"That's weird," said Sarah, inspecting her own amulet. "Mine's just black and icky looking."

"They're different for everyone," said Mop.

Slipping her amulet back into her pocket, Sarah asked Mop how well he knew her parents. "They never mentioned you."

"Met them after the war. Have flown them all over the place. North and South America, the Caribbean. Last I heard they were in Africa. Then I got that message asking me to pick you guys up and take you to Wildeor."

Alex perked up at the mention of Wildeor. "Is that where we're headed? Wildeor? The place I'm supposed to be, you know . . . king of?"

"Lord, Alex," said Sarah.

"Lord Alex. I like that. Has a nice ring to it."

Mop laughed. "Yup, we're headed for Wildeor all right. Not an easy place to get to. Been a secret so long, I'm not sure anyone could find it without help. By the way, Sarah, where's that package you rescued from that nasty old Pudsley woman?"

During the excitement of their escape from Mortimer's Point, Sarah had hastily thrown everything she'd been carrying, including the package, into the floatplane. Scrambling around on her hands and knees, she eventually found it wedged under a gas canister. She unwrapped the package and discovered a small, leather-bound book that looked as if it'd been through a few adventures of its own.

As she flicked through the pages, Alex could see it was full of tidy diagrams, charts, and notes—quite the opposite to his own journals, which were always crammed full of notes, sketches, and scraps of newspapers and magazines. As Sarah held the book up to show Mop, a note fell from its pages. She read it out loud:

ADDIS ABABA, JUNE 30TH, 1929

DEAREST SARAH,
WE'VE ARRANGED FOR A PILOT TO PICK YOU UP. LONNIE DONNELLY. TRUST HIM. HE HAS ALSO BEEN INSTRUCTED TO PICK UP A BOY, ALEX. YOU MAY REMEMBER HIM AS THE SAD-LOOKING LITTLE FELLOW WHO LIVED NEXT DOOR WITH MRS. PUDSLEY.
MR. DONNELLY WILL TAKE YOU WHERE YOU WILL BE SAFE. IT IS A LONG TRIP, NOT WITHOUT ITS DANGERS. (DO NOT OVERPACK—TRAVEL LIGHT!)

Mop chortled. "Bit late for that!"

"Yes, but what about the bit where you're supposed to make this sorry expedition to who-knows-where a safe one?" responded Sarah before continuing to read:

YOU MAY NOT HEAR FROM US FOR A WHILE, BUT SO LONG AS YOU ARE SAFE, WE WILL BE, TOO. STICK CLOSE TO ALEX. HE IS NOT AS WORLDLY WISE AS YOU, AND KNOWS NOTHING OF HIS ROLE IN THE STRUGGLE

THAT IS AHEAD.

KEEP THIS BOOK SAFE. IT CONTAINS INFORMATION THE ULTIMA DESPERATELY NEEDS. IF IT FALLS INTO THEIR HANDS, OR IF THEY CAPTURE ALEX, EVERYTHING WILL BE UNDONE, AND ALL OUR LIVES WILL BE AT RISK. DELIVER IT TO OUR FRIEND MR. LIAT. HE'LL HELP YOU, ALTHOUGH HE HAS BEEN UNUSUALLY SILENT OF LATE.

YOUR LOVING PARENTS

Sarah looked at Mop, clearly confused by the letter. "Are they OK?"

"They know how to look after themselves," said Mop.

Alex turned to offer Sarah some encouragement of his own only to find her staring off into the distance, a troubled expression on her face as she toyed with a slender gold ring on her finger. "They'll be OK," he said reassuringly. "Remember what they said: if we stick together, everything will work out fine."

Leaving Sarah alone with her thoughts, Alex turned his attention back to Mop.

"The supply plane'll be here soon, so keep your eyes peeled," instructed Mop. "It should be coming in from the west. Uh, no . . . your other west, Alex."

Mop went on to explain how a giant flying boat was being tested as a supply plane for the *Graf Zeppelin*, a German airship about to embark on its first around-the-world flight. Known as the Dornier Do-X, the supply plane had arrived in New York ahead of the Zeppelin. Mop had no problem convincing the pilot, an adventurer much like himself, to participate in the refuelling experiment.

Alex was thrilled at the news of the Do-X's connection to the Zeppelin. He was fascinated by the huge airships, and so was determined to be the first to see its supply plane. Scanning the horizon eagerly with Mop's binoculars, he was rewarded soon after as the unmistakable shape of an aircraft loomed into view. "Wow, it's huge! I can see . . . um . . . yes, twelve engines. Holy cow, it really does look like a ship!"

"Sounds about right," said Mop, banking the floatplane toward the lumbering giant, and spelling out what was expected of everyone. Alex, naturally, took notes:

- Sarah to secure safety rope around Alex (me) anchored at the rear of the floatplane
- Mop to position floatplane directly underneath Do-X
- Do-X's crew to lower fuel line to the floatplane
- Securely anchored, Alex (me) to lean out (carefully), grab fuel line, and place in fuel tank
- Signal supply plane to start pumping

Sarah, it soon became clear, was less than confident about their chances of success. Mop smiled broadly as he reassured her of his plan's simplicity. "Just make sure that rope is anchored properly, and everything will be copacetic."

Eagerly pushing open the passenger door, Alex was ready before Sarah had even picked up the safety rope. Positioning herself behind him, she fastened the rope to the boat anchor used to moor the plane in shallow water, then tied the other end around his waist.

"This is the second time today I've had to stop you from falling off something!" she hollered over the din of wind and engines.

Alex turned and smiled, then stretched his arms out wide, as if about to take flight. "I feel like a bird!"

"You're insane!" she replied. "Whose side is he on, anyway? We've only known him a few hours and he's already tried killing us three times. Now here we go again!"

Alex watched excitedly as they took up their position beneath the massive supply plane. Holding onto the door frame, he stretched as far as he could in an attempt to catch the fuel line as it swung about erratically.

"I can't reach it! I'm going to try to get closer!"

34

Before Sarah could protest, Alex stepped onto the float. Grabbing hold of the wing strut, he stretched forward to grab the fuel line as it swung toward him. With lightning reflexes, he lunged at the line, this time successfully. Placing the nozzle into the fuel tank, he waved his arm to signal the supply plane to commence pumping, all the while placing as much pressure as possible on the nozzle to maintain the connection.

The ten minutes needed to transfer the fuel was almost up when Alex noticed a crew member on the huge aircraft waving frantically and pointing at the skyline behind them. His heart skipped a beat as he made out the silhouette of another floatplane heading their way. Struggling to remove the nozzle, he began to panic when he realized it was stuck and wouldn't budge. Thinking more leverage was needed, he positioned himself behind the nozzle and heaved with all his strength. At that exact moment, both planes hit a wall of turbulence that yanked the nozzle free.

As the turbulence tossed the two aircraft about, the fuel line swung back toward Alex. Thrashing around like a snake, it became entangled with the safety rope Sarah had placed around his waist. Before he could react, a sharp tug on the fuel line hauled him violently off his perch, leaving him dangling helplessly from the supply plane like a fish on a line. Worse still, the heavy anchor Sarah had mistakenly thought would secure him had been pulled out of the floatplane and now swung from his waist, squeezing his stomach like a vice.

His heart pounding, Alex watched as Mop's floatplane banked hard to the left. Kicking his legs wildly, he was able to keep the aircraft in sight as it completed a tight 360-degree turn and positioned itself directly beneath him. He held his breath as the anchor narrowly avoided banging into the propeller, crashing against the windscreen before finally coming to rest between the wings. Seconds later, Mop opened the small skylight in the fuselage and, as agile as an acrobat, climbed onto the roof. Standing just a few feet below, he was almost able to grab Alex's feet.

"Unhook the nozzle, I'll catch you! Hurry!"

Alex needed no convincing and worked feverishly to unhook the fuel line. Finally free, he fell onto the fuselage in front of Mop, who leapt forward just in time to catch the anchor rope, stopping it from sliding off the floatplane and taking Alex with it. Pulling a knife from his pocket, Mop cut the rope, letting the anchor crash into the trees far below.

"You OK?" asked Mop.

"I . . . think so," said Alex, as he clung to the roof of the aircraft, scared to even move in case he fell.

"Don't ever try any barnstorming tricks like that again, you hear? At least not until you've had some practice!"

Alex managed a faint smile as Mop gave the Do-X the all clear. Grabbing Alex's hand and leading him to the skylight, Mop helped him climb inside before relieving Sarah of her duties in the cockpit.

"Good job, Sarah. We'll make a pilot out of you yet! But honey, why didn't you anchor the rope like I told you?"

"Anchor it? I thought you said tie it to the anchor!"

"Jeez, and you said I was trying to kill you guys."

"Mop," said Alex once he'd caught his breath. "You knew that supply plane was a flying boat, right?"

"Course I did."

"Then why didn't we just land on the lake and refuel?"

"Heck, where's the fun in that."

"Hey guys, we've got company!" shouted Sarah, pointing at the Ultima floatplane closing in on them, so close now they could make out the pilot's features. "Where on earth do they get those guys? They all look like movie stars."

"Evil movie stars," quipped Alex.

"Those aren't even the bad ones," said Mop. "They'd be shooting at—"

A burst of gunfire whizzed past the floatplane. "Probably just a warning! If they wanted to bring us down, they'd shoot directly at the plane."

A second burst of gunfire was followed by the metallic clink-clink of bullets hitting the side of the Travelair. Mop banked sharply away from their pursuers to avoid further gunfire.

"I could throw some suitcases at them," said Alex.

"No need. That old plane of theirs is built for distance, not speed.

We'll lose them soon enough now it's getting dark. You guys better get some rest. You've got another crazy long day ahead of you tomorrow."

"Oh, great," said Sarah sarcastically. "I guess that means I'll have to cancel my afternoon at the beauty parlour?"

"You betcha," said Mop. "It's going to be a while before either of you see any home comforts. So get used to roughing it."

Unlike Sarah, Alex certainly felt no remorse about leaving his previous existence behind. "Are you serious? I won't have to go back to Mrs. Pudsley?"

"Not for now, anyway," said Mop. "I don't know exactly what's in store for you guys, but I've a hunch things will never be the same."

CHAPTER 5

THE NOT-SO-FRIENDLY GIANT

Alex awoke with a start. They were no longer flying, and the constant drone of the engine had been replaced by the sound of water lapping gently against the aircraft's floats. Sarah lay close by, having made a somewhat lumpy bed out of the luggage and backpacks at the rear of the plane. Alex's makeshift bed extended into the washroom, and he failed to avoid smacking his head against the small sink as he sat upright. Mop was nowhere to be seen.

The first signs of daylight crept over the tree line on the far side of the lake. Alex could see they'd landed close to the base of a range of mountains, which rose out of the dense forest, their snow-crowned peaks shrouded in cloud.

Alarmed by the sound of someone—or some thing—splashing toward him from the shoreline, Alex reached into the cockpit for the wrench Mop used for repairs, just in case he needed it to defend himself. Peering into the early morning mist, he could make out the silhouette of a bulky figure lumbering his way.

"Mop?" he said nervously. "Is that you?"

"You better hope so," came the reply.

Alex watched groggily as Mop plunked two heavy gas cans into the shallow water beside the plane. "Where'd you find that?"

"When you fly over bush country as much as I do, you stash a few cans away here and there. Never know when you're going to need them."

"You've been here before?"

Mop smiled as he hoisted the first can high enough to pour its contents into the floatplane. "Oh, once or twice."

Hearing a noise behind him, Alex turned to see Sarah stretching and yawning before joining him up front. "Mop, did you ever bring Mom and Dad up here?" she asked.

"A few times. They liked it here. Always said they were looking forward to introducing you to Wildeor. Now you'll just have to do it on your own."

Alex wasn't sure he liked what he heard. "You're not coming with us?"

"Nope. This is where you start walking."

"We're walking to Wildeor?"

"Yup. Those mountains are far too dangerous to fly over. See that mist? Thick as molasses. We wouldn't see anything until we hit it. A few crazy flyboys have tried. No one ever saw them again. Tom and I have been working on a system to control the clouds to make it safe for us good guys to come and go. Until then, the only way in is on foot. Everything you need for the two-day trek is inside those backpacks, including flashlights."

Sarah gasped. "That long?"

"If you don't get lost."

"And if we do?" she asked.

"Just stick to the trail," said Mop. "Don't deviate from it and you'll be OK. That's crucial, understand?"

"Understood," said Alex. "You're definitely not coming with us?"

"Afraid not, kiddo. Places to go, people to see."

Alex could barely hide his disappointment at the news. "What . . . what about, um, keeping us safe, you know, like . . . like Sarah's parents asked you to do?"

The moment he'd finished pouring the last of the gas, Mop placed a reassuring hand on Alex's shoulder. "If I didn't think you and Sarah could handle the journey alone, do you think I'd leave you? I have a hunch you'll make it to Wildeor without incident."

"Couldn't we stay with you? Maybe help you find Sarah's parents?"

"Not possible, sorry. I've got other stuff needs doing first. And based on what we already know about those Ultima guys, I'll have my hands full getting ready for my next run-in with them."

Mop pointed to a clearing in the otherwise dense forest further along the shoreline. Marking the entrance of the trail to Wildeor was a primitive stone statue as tall as a house.

"Wow! That's one big inuksuk!" said Alex.

"Sort of," replied Mop. "It's actually called an inunnguaq because it has arms and legs."

"In a . . . what?" asked Sarah.

"In-unn-guaq. It means sweet little man, though they're usually a lot smaller than that guy. Funny, I remember it being on the other side of that clearing. Oh, by the way, be sure to keep those amulets on you at all times. In case you run into any beasts."

"Beasts?" said Sarah. "You mean, with teeth and claws, or cute and cuddly?"

"Both. Sometimes all in the same package."

Mop suddenly motioned them to be silent. Seconds later, Alex heard the distant drone of an approaching engine, followed soon after by the appearance of a floatplane.

"Is it them?" asked Sarah.

"Has to be. Get your stuff."

Sarah moaned as she turned to help Alex retrieve their gear from the rear of the plane. "Did you never think to choose a less visible colour scheme for this old heap? Bright orange and yellow are a tad conspicuous, don't you think?"

"Seemed like a good idea when I got it," said Mop. "Easier to spot if I ever went down. Course, had I known it'd make a good target, I'd have gone for something a little more discrete."

Passing the backpacks to Alex, Sarah then slid her biggest suitcase forward for Mop to unload.

The pilot shook his head in disbelief. "Tell me you're not serious?"

"If you think I'm going to traipse through this . . . this jungle . . . without my personal belongings, you're very much mistaken. Anyway, I've only packed the essentials."

The Ultima aircraft had now reached the lake, and Alex watched anxiously as it descended, its floats skimming the surface of the water for a few seconds before it touched down and turned toward the Travelair. Alex helped push the floatplane into deeper water, and Mop was soon aboard and firing up the engine. Beckoning Alex closer, he shouted a few last words of advice. "Stick to the trails, and keep those amulets on! And tell Sarah not to worry. I'll find her parents."

As Alex splashed back to shore, Mop shouted a final farewell and a few words of caution. Although he couldn't decipher much of what was said over the noise of the engine, Alex did manage to catch a few words: "Watch . . . cave . . . Wendy . . . careful! See ya . . . "

Alex watched with a sinking feeling as Mop gunned the Travelair's engine and steered straight toward the enemy.

"What was all that about?" shouted Sarah over the racket made by the two aircraft.

"No idea. All I heard was something about someone called Wendy, and a cave."

"He's crazy," she said.

"He knows what he's doing . . . I think," said Alex, crossing his fingers as Mop raced toward the Ultima in a deadly game of chicken. Just as a collision looked inevitable, the Travelair lurched upwards, its floats smacking the tail of the Ultima aircraft with a dull thud, sheering off its rudder.

Alex watched in awe as Mop circled back toward the damaged floatplane. As the Travelair skimmed low over the water toward the Ultima, Alex whooped excitedly as the crew panicked and jumped overboard.

"I am so going to learn to fly!"

"If you live that long," remarked Sarah. "Who's Wendy, anyway?"

"Guess we'll find out soon enough," he said, shouldering his backpack and helping Sarah with hers. Grabbing the heavy suitcase, he made his way as quickly as possible to the stone giant, only stopping long enough to read a crudely painted sign placed upon it: I'D TURN BACK IF I WERE YOU!

Sarah wasn't impressed. "If that's someone's idea of a joke, it's pretty lame."

The sign was soon forgotten as gunshots rang out across the lake. With bullets ricocheting around them, Alex pushed Sarah into the shelter of the trees. The wide, zigzagging trail looked as if it'd been made by a tank. Smaller trees and bushes were crushed flat, and some of the larger varieties—pine, maple and oak—had been snapped off at the trunk. Still others had been ripped right out of the ground.

Rounding a bend in the trail, a second sign provided another excuse to catch their breath. This one read: WARNING! TRESPASSERS WILL BE EATEN.

"Very funny," said Sarah. "Listen, if all those goons want is that notebook, let's leave it on the trail for them. Maybe they'll stop bothering us."

"We can't do that! Remember what your parents said? We have to get that book to Tom. And we'd get there a heck of a lot quicker if we dumped this case. What's in it, a body?"

Sarah smiled. "What, and let those animals have my stuff? It's OK for you men. You live in the same clothes for weeks on end. I'm . . . we're different. A girl needs a change of outfit. New shoes. A few simple luxuries, that sort of thing."

"OK, fine. I'll take it if it makes you happy. Let's just get out of here!"

The sound of shouting and barking spurred Alex into action. He yelled at Sarah to hurry and, with her luggage in hand, kept pace with her in spite of the extra load. Fear gripped them as their pursuers closed in. They hadn't gone far when Sarah stumbled, twisting her foot as she tripped over a fallen tree. She grimaced as she tried to place weight on her sprained ankle.

Only a bend in the trail now separated them from the Ultima. Realizing Sarah couldn't get away quickly enough, Alex placed himself in front of her and braced for the worst. Then, unexpectedly, the ground trembled as if an earthquake had struck, and the dense foliage around them shook violently. At the same time, the air filled with the sharp cracking sound of stone smacking hard against stone, as well as sporadic gunfire and shouting.

As suddenly as it began, it was all over. An eerie stillness descended, followed by the return of normal forest sounds—of birds chirping, and a gentle breeze fluttering through branches. Then a rustling in the bushes nearby once again had Alex fearing the worst. Picking up a rock, he braced himself for whatever was headed their way.

"Like that's going to help," said Sarah.

They both jumped when a dog crashed unexpectedly through the dense undergrowth. Soaked in blood, it paid no attention to them as it brushed past hurriedly and limped down the trail, ears back and tail between its legs.

Sarah gasped in shock. "What could possibly have done that?"

"No idea," said Alex. "But it must be one of the Ultima's dogs." Relieved that the danger seemed to have passed for the time being, he dropped the rock and turned his attention to Sarah's injury. "How's that foot?"

"I'll manage."

Snapping a branch from a fallen tree, Alex checked it for strength and handed it to Sarah. "Of course you will. But this'll help."

Sarah took the makeshift crutch gratefully, then reached out for Alex's hand. "Just to keep me steady," she said.

Their progress now was slow, but it wasn't long before they heard the welcome burbling of fast-flowing water ahead. Mop had told them to follow the river upstream into the mountains, and so the sound reassured Alex that they were heading in the right direction.

They'd just reached the river when the whimpering of a distressed animal caught their attention. Motioning Sarah to stay put, Alex crept cautiously toward the rapids, wielding the makeshift crutch like a baseball bat in case he met anything unpleasant. The whining came from the wounded dog which was lying helpless on the riverbank, panting hard as it struggled for breath. Kneeling beside it, Alex was struck by its unusual appearance—as big as a Doberman, it had a wild, wolf-like look about it, sleek and strong and built to hunt.

Alex loosened the coarse leather collar around its neck to help it breathe. Sensing the boy posed no threat, the once aggressive dog wagged its tail feebly.

"Steady, fella. It's not your fault. They made you that way, didn't they?"

Calmed by Alex's soothing voice, the dog ceased its whimpering. Cupping his hands in the cool water of the river, he offered the animal a drink. It lapped the water greedily, tickling his palms with its rough tongue. Scooping up more water, Alex attempted to wash away the blood and grime that was caked around its face.

So engrossed was he in the fate of the dog that he didn't at first notice Sarah's presence. "Let's go, Alex. You can't help it now."

Alex said nothing, cradling the dog's head as it drew its final breath.

"Alex?"

Alex didn't move. He was mesmerized by the appearance of a faint, shapeless white shadow that rose from the dog's body and hung in the air over its corpse. Oddly, he was filled with an unusual sense of peace, and couldn't help smiling as the shadow melted away like a morning mist.

"What's so funny?" asked Sarah. "The poor thing's dead, and you're smiling. It's freaking me out."

"Didn't you see it?"

"See what?"

Alex hesitated, uncertain Sarah would understand. He said nothing. Picking up the lifeless body, he placed it at the foot of a large maple tree and attempted to scrape away enough soil for a grave. But it was too rocky to dig, so he covered the body with leaves instead.

"Do you think they're all dead?" asked Sarah. She'd removed the hiking boots Mop had given her and was massaging her injured ankle.

"Must be. Maybe whatever it was that stopped them is on our side."

"Our side? This isn't a game! We could have been killed. Again!"

Alex ignored Sarah's comment as he knelt down to inspect her ankle. "At least it's not broken. We need something to bind it."

Alex pulled out his pocketknife and set about cutting the left sleeve off his shirt before tearing the material into strips. Placing Sarah's foot in his lap, he wrapped the improvised bandage around her ankle. Passing it under the sole, he repeated the process until satisfied it would provide at least temporary support.

"Not bad for a country boy," said Sarah.

Alex gave the bandage a tug, causing her to wince.

"Ow! Hey, I was just kidding," she said. "What do you think attacked them?"

"You'll probably just laugh if I told you what I think."

"Try me."

Alex perched himself on a rock jutting into the river. Sliding off his boots, he slipped his tired feet into the chilly water. "I think it was the stone man."

As predicted, Sarah laughed. "Are you crazy?"

"All that noise, the ground shaking. That thing was gigantic!"

"That's ridiculous. It's simply not possible. Is it?"

"What else could have stopped a bunch of armed thugs like that?"

Sarah thought for a moment. "I guess a stone giant makes about as much sense as anything else after everything we've seen so far."

Alex swished his tired feet in the water, enjoying the soothing sensation of the cool water on his skin. "Something saved us. I'm sure Tom will have a perfectly reasonable explanation for everything."

"What makes you so sure he can help?"

"Just a hunch."

Sarah pulled her hiking boot back on. "Now you sound like Mop. Nice guy, but not much use in the predication department. What was it he said? 'I have a hunch you'll make it to Wildeor without incident?' Yeah, right. Then there was, 'I don't make promises I can't keep.' What a jerk."

Alex lifted his feet out of the river and swung around to face Sarah.

"At least he was right about the route to Wildeor being easy to follow. There's the path," he said, pointing to the well-worn trail following the river upstream. "Shouldn't be too hard."

"What, apart from dealing with that huge mountain?" scoffed Sarah. "Easy enough with one good leg. Boys! You're all the same. Always looking for adventure. All I want is to go home, have a nice cup of tea and a bath."

"I could probably do the tea thing," said Alex, grabbing his backpack and rummaging through their food supplies. "Well, I would if we had tea. And a kettle. Or teapot. A stove. Some milk. And sugar. Do you take sugar? I'd need that, too."

"Oh, brother," said Sarah.

"Will water do?"

CHAPTER 6

RELICS AND RIVALS

Standing stock still in front of the huge waterfall, Alex was mesmerized by the cool mist rising from the dark water as it thundered into the pool far below. Sarah plunked herself down beside him, making a seat of the suitcase he'd been carrying for her. "Now what, smarty pants?"

They'd spent the day climbing steadily upriver to the base of the fog-shrouded mountain only to find their way blocked by the waterfall—as high, Sarah claimed, as the new Chrysler Building being built in New York. It was a reference lost on Alex, who'd never seen a city, let alone a skyscraper. "All we've got to do is find a way around it. Or over it. Maybe . . . maybe even through it," he said. "Yes, through it might just work."

Sarah, however, wasn't interested in the mountain. "They'll be OK, won't they?" she finally asked.

"Who?"

"My parents."

Her characteristic self-confidence was, for a moment, replaced by a vulnerability Alex found unsettling—almost as unsettling as her appearance. Her blazing red hair was a straggly strawlike mess. Gone was the tidy clothing, replaced by oversized denim pants and a flannel shirt Mop had given her. It was grass-stained and dirty after a day on the run. She looked, thought Alex, like a messed-up Anne of Green Gables.

"Of course," he said as convincingly as possible. "Mop will fetch them home, just wait and see."

Sarah said nothing more on the topic, so Alex again turned his attention to the issue of the waterfall and getting to Wildeor. Then, with a flash of inspiration, he grabbed Sarah's hand. "That's it! You ready?"

"Ready for what, exactly?"

Hauling her to her feet and picking up the suitcase, Alex leapt through the icy cold water, dragging the protesting Sarah with him. Soaking wet and shivering, Alex turned on his flashlight and was relieved to find they were standing in a dark, cold cave.

Sarah, looking like a drowned rat, was considerably less thrilled. "Are you crazy?"

Alex ignored her complaints. "Ever read *Last of the Mohicans*? Worked for them . . . This has to be the way into Wildeor. It's where the trail led. And Mop did say something about a cave."

"He also said something about a Wendy," said Sarah. "But there sure as heck is no Wendy in here!" Snatching the suitcase huffily, she placed it on the ground and rummaged for something dry to wear. "You'd better change, Alex," she said, throwing a dry shirt his way. "You'll catch your death of cold."

Sarah let out a small gasp as Alex pulled off the sopping wet garment. "Oh my . . what's that?" Before he could respond, she stepped forward and placed her hand gently on the unusual markings on his back. Alex jumped at the unexpected touch.

"Hey, your hand's cold!" he said, quickly pulling on the shirt. "They're just birthmarks . . . no big deal."

"They look more like scars."

Sarah was right. Three scars as thick as fingers stretched diagonally across his back from his right shoulder to his left hip. He had no idea how he got them, but he'd had them for as long as he could remember. In his rush to cover up his disfigurement, he tripped over something soft on the damp cave floor. It was a rolled-up canvas sheet the size of a pillow. Attached to it was a piece of paper, yellow with age.

Alex was grateful for the opportunity to change the subject. "It's a boat. Says here: 'Halkett's Boat-cloak. Inflated, carries two. Deflated, serves as a waterproof cloak. Patent Pending, 1844.'"

Halkett's Boat-Cloak

What Alex didn't tell Sarah was that the boat-cloak looked about as seaworthy as a brick. He also didn't say anything about the fact its pockets contained a small bellows to inflate it, or that it came with a walking stick that doubled as a paddle. And he certainly didn't mention the umbrella that also served as a sail.

Thinking the unusual vessel might come in handy, Alex slung the boat-cloak over his shoulder and again turning his attention to the cave's murky interior. Although the powerful beam of his flashlight sliced through the inky blackness like a miniature searchlight, he could see no end to it. Shining the light onto the jagged walls, he traced the beam upward, mesmerized by the dancing shadows cast by the outcrops of rock.

A well-worn pathway led deeper into the cave. But something made Alex feel uneasy. It wasn't just the impenetrable gloom, or the increasingly strong smell of damp soil and decay. It was an unsettling feeling that they weren't alone. Picking their way carefully along the trail, they cringed as each gravelly footstep echoed loudly around them.

"Gosh, I hope that terrible smell isn't you?" said Sarah in disgust, screwing up her nose.

"Not this time," said Alex, holding his fingers to his nose to block the sickly sweet smell of decay that seemed to grow stronger the deeper they went.

It wasn't long before Alex's attention was drawn to something glimmering in the beam of the flashlight a short distance from the pathway. Torn between sticking to the trail or making a detour, he eventually coaxed a reluctant Sarah to investigate the source of his curiosity. What they found were heaps of old uniforms and innumerable tattered shoes and boots, grey with dust. Another smaller mound consisted of assorted armour and weapons, including swords, pikes, and guns ranging from ancient muskets to more modern pistols and rifles. Most of them, Alex noted, looked as if they'd seen their fair share of action.

Pulling an old spiked steel helmet from the jumble of armour, Sarah placed it on Alex's head. "I wonder how all this stuff got here?" she asked.

"Sure didn't get here on its own," said Alex, straightening the helmet and reaching for a small ivory-handled revolver that caught his eye. He was intrigued by the name BRITISH BULL DOG engraved on the chamber. With hardly a second thought, he placed the weapon in his backpack. He proceeded cautiously around the collection of weapons only to find himself dwarfed by a mass of bones stacked high against the side of the cave.

"Are they human?" Sarah whispered, her voice muffled by the handkerchief she held to her face. "That smell! It's like rotten meat, only worse."

Alex pulled a long bone—bleached white and picked clean—from the immense pile. "It must be some kind of burial ground. Strange . . . no skulls."

"Wrong," said Sarah, shining her flashlight higher up the wall of the cave.

What Alex had mistaken for rocks were, in fact, human skulls. Set in deep alcoves, row upon row of grisly skulls stretched as far as he could see in every direction.

Frightened, Sarah grabbed his arm. "Let's get out of here. I don't want to end up part of some horrible bone collection!"

Alex delicately placed the bone back where he'd found it and turned to rejoin her. He hadn't gone more than a few feet when the whole mountain of bones came clattering down. It sounded like a million marbles had been sent clacking across the stone floor.

"So much for being quiet," said Sarah when the din finally subsided.

Alex motioned her to be quiet. "Did you hear that? Like thunder, only—" Alex stopped mid-sentence, interrupted by the same loud, low rumbling he'd heard moments earlier. The stench also grew stronger.

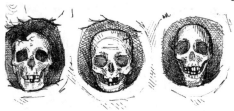

"That's just rotten," said Sarah, covering her face with her sleeve.

Alex choked back tears as the odour worsened, a smell of death and decay so strong it stung his nostrils. "Why do I get this horrible feeling we're not alone?" he asked as he tried to retrace his steps. Problem was, more than one narrow path led away from their gruesome discovery, and he felt a twinge of panic when he failed to recognize the one leading to the main trail. Finding no clear route, Alex eventually decided to do as Mop had suggested—when in doubt, follow your nose.

Leading Sarah away from the rancid smell of decay, their progress at first seemed slow. But as the minutes turned to hours, he became increasingly aware that the cave seemed to be closing in on them, its walls pressing in so closely he could reach out and touch either side.

Alex stopped abruptly, causing Sarah to crash into him. They'd come to the end of the cave.

"We're lost, aren't we?" she asked.

Exhausted, Alex dropped to the ground, burying his head in his hands, ashamed at having led them off course and worried they might not be alone. "I'm . . . I'm sorry, Sarah. I shouldn't have left the trail."

Sarah sat down next to him. "It's not your fault," she said. "At least, it's not all your fault. This is as much my parent's fault as anyone's."

Alex picked up a pebble and threw it at the end of the tunnel. "We shouldn't blame anyone, really . . . it's just the way it is." Picking up a handful of pebbles, he found comfort in the reassuring *plink-thunk* sound they made as they bounced off the wall and onto the ground. After a few minutes, he stopped. Something about the noise they made wasn't quite right. Reaching for a slightly larger rock, he threw it hard against the cave wall. To his delight, he was rewarded with a hollow thunk.

Picking up an even larger rock, Alex bashed it against the side of the cave. "Hear that? It's hollow!" A few swipes later and he was rewarded by the sound of crumbling stone as a small hole appeared, bringing with it a faint trace of fresh air. Sarah joined in, as excited as he was about the discovery of a potential exit. It wasn't long before they'd made a hole big enough to squeeze through.

Stopping to survey their handiwork, Sarah gave Alex a pat on the back. "I suppose you read that in a book, too?"

Alex shook his head. "Nope. Pure chance. But I sure hope it'll get us away from whatever it is that's following us."

Alarmed, Sarah shone her flashlight back along the trail. "We're being followed?" she asked nervously. Stepping backward, she accidentally knocked Alex's flashlight out of his hand. They watched helplessly as it disappeared down the hole.

"Must be some kind of tunnel," he said, peeking into the opening. "Would you like to go first?"

"No, no, after you. We're all equals in my book."

Alex shrugged off his backpack and tossed it into the hole along with the boat-cloak, then jumped in after them. His slide down the surprisingly well-worn shaft was brief but bumpy, and seconds later he found himself lying in a dusty heap on the ground of a much smaller cavern. A whooshing sound announced the arrival of the suitcase, followed, seconds later, by Sarah as she piled on top of him.

"Did you plan that?" asked Alex as he quickly disentangled himself from her.

"No, but sure was nice having something soft to land on! Apart from this," she added, passing the pointy helmet back to Alex.

Helping Sarah to her feet, Alex picked up the flashlight and tried to get his bearings. The room appeared to be a crypt, and was dominated by a large stone tomb in the centre. Six smaller, less ornate tombs were set in a circle around it.

Approaching the largest tomb, Alex could see images carved into it of creatures both real and imaginary, including winged horses, dragons, and sea serpents. At the end of it stood a large stone in which a small sword was buried. All that could be seen of the weapon was its worn leather grip and an inch or two of dull blade. Alex found himself drawn to the sword, and for some inexplicable reason reached out and clasped the grip in his hand. Without any effort whatsoever, he removed the sword as easily as if the rock had been butter. The sword was only as long as his forearm and was unusually plain, devoid of anything that might suggest it had once belonged to anyone of importance.

"Let's get out of here," called Sarah from the other end of the crypt. "This place gives me the shivers."

Tucking the sword carefully into his belt, Alex reluctantly followed Sarah to the large door at the far end of the room. Above the heavy wooden structure was an inscription that read: DOMNE WILDEOR.

"That's what's on my watch!"

Sarah grasped the metal door handle and twisted it. Try as she might, she was unable to open it. "I think it's locked."

Alex placed his shoulder against the ancient door and gave it a shove. To his surprise, the wood panels, rotten with age, gave way. Sarah was through the door and jogging down the large hallway before Alex could even get to his feet. "Hurry, there's our way out!" she hollered, pointing to a small patch of light shining through an archway at the far end of the cavernous corridor.

Passing row upon row of huge wooden doors just like the one he'd destroyed, Alex was tempted to find out what lay behind them. Instead, he continued toward the light, spurred on by the same thunderous rumbling they'd heard earlier. Only now it was closer.

Pushing past Alex, Sarah ducked through the small archway leading to the stairs at the end of the corridor. "Forget everything I said earlier. It's women and children first. That's me on both counts!"

"Glad to see you haven't lost your sense of humour," muttered Alex as he caught up to Sarah.

The stairs were small and protruded from the walls like broken teeth as they spiralled up a wide chimney-like shaft. Out of curiosity, Alex kicked a small rock into the dark void below, waiting expectantly for it to hit the bottom. He heard nothing.

The sound of something large scraping past the entrance to the crude stairway caused him to swing around in time to catch a glimpse of a large, human-like figure gliding past the tiny opening. "I think we've got company!" he said in a panic, pushing Sarah toward the stairs. He could tell the creature was too big to enter the stairwell, and hoped there was no other way in.

After what seemed an eternity climbing the stairs, Sarah stopped for a rest at an opening about halfway up the shaft.

"I wonder if that was Wendy?" asked Alex. "Do you think we lost it?"

A scraping sound behind them was all the answer he needed. Shining his flashlight down the short passageway, Alex revealed two large gnarly hands, their long skinny fingers oozing with decay, clawing desperately at a mound of boulders blocking the entrance. Almost immediately the hands disappeared, only to be replaced by the gaunt, withered face of the horrific monster, its almost translucent skin pulled tightly over its bony skull. Its hungry eyes were set deep in their sockets, and what lips it had were drawn tightly over decaying gums and teeth. It looked as if it had risen from the dead.

To Alex's surprise, Sarah grabbed her suitcase, hobbled to within a few yards of the creature and flung the heavy case at it, hitting it square on the mouth. With an ear-piercing screech, the monster recoiled as the suitcase struck home, splitting its gnarly bottom lip. Falling to the ground, the suitcase split open, revealing amidst the clothes and make-up a collection of small electrical appliances including an iron and a hairdryer.

Alex grimaced. "Darn it, Sarah! Now he's really mad! Hopefully it'll find some of that junk I've been lugging around for you useful!"

Motivated by the sound of the hideous monster scrabbling furiously to break through the stone barrier, they hurried up the stairs as fast as their legs would carry them. Then, with less than fifty yards to go, the sound suddenly stopped. Alex looked back to see the creature poke its head out of the smaller tunnel as it looked about for its prey.

"What does it want?" shouted Sarah.

"Dinner!"

"Well, it's not getting me!" she shouted, hurling her flashlight at it.

"Will you please stop throwing things at it! You're just making it angrier!"

Clawing its way frantically toward them, the monster pulled its ugly, bony frame upwards as nimble as a spider. A trace of sunlight sliced through the darkness that had enveloped them since they'd entered the monster's lair so many hours earlier. Alex, squinting as his eyes adjusted to the light, removed the steel helmet Sarah had given him and threw it at the creature, catching it on the head with a metallic *thwack*.

But it wasn't enough to stop the hideous creature from gaining on him. Reaching up and grabbing his ankle, it tried to pull him back down the shaft. The stomach-churning stench of rotting meat all but overcame Alex as a searing pain shot up his leg. Worse still, the monster spat at him; he ducked just in time to avoid a large ball of bile, which hit the cave wall just inches from his head. He watched in horror as the bile burned into the rock with a loud hiss.

"Quick! Take my hand!" shouted Sarah. Alex grabbed her hand only to be caught in a deadly tug-of-war. Reaching for the small sword with his free hand, he slashed the blade across the creature's forearm, but the creature didn't relax its grip. He swung the sword again. This time the force of the blow severed the tip of one of the creature's fingers. Howling in pain, it relaxed its grip long enough for Alex to yank his foot free and scramble up the remaining stairs to safety.

Standing panting in the warm, welcoming sunshine, the two friends now watched, terrified, as the creature prepared to climb out of the tunnel. Fixing them with its hateful gaze, it wiped the drool from its mouth as it contemplated who to tear apart first.

CHAPTER 7

WILD ABOUT WILDEOR

A sudden crash of rock shattered the tension just as the cave creature prepared to pounce. An avalanche of boulders had toppled off the mountainside and was now hurtling toward them at breakneck speed. Pushing Sarah out of the way, Alex only just managed to jump clear as the enormous pile of stones crashed onto the entrance to the monster's lair, sealing it shut.

Scrambling to her feet, Sarah surveyed the scene in disbelief. "Was it me, or did that pile of rocks look like that innu-thing?"

"It sure did," said Alex, still shaking from his ordeal. All he could think about was the searing pain in his leg. The pant leg was burnt clean through—the hair on his flesh singed away, the skin blistered and sore.

Sarah knelt beside him to inspect the wound. "I think I'm going to need that other sleeve," she said.

Alex passed her his penknife, and she was soon wrapping the makeshift bandage around the injury while he gritted his teeth. Once she'd finished, Alex made his way to the ledge overlooking Wildeor.

"Wow! It's incredible!" he said breathlessly as he took in the remarkable view.

"It certainly is," said Sarah in wonderment as she joined him. "Truly beautiful."

Wildeor was well named, Alex thought. Untouched by man or machine, it was a place where nature had been left to its own devices. Majestic maple, oak, pine, and fir spread out densely in all directions, their towering canopy rising hundreds of feet in the air. Flocks of colourful birds flitted from treetop to treetop, or skimmed over the long finger lake that cut a swath through the endless sea of green. Stretching far into the distance, the lake was at least a mile wide in places, and many more miles long. Here and there, small islands—some treed, others just small outcrops of rock—peaked out of the water. The whole vast area was bordered by the tall, cloud-covered mountains they observed the previous day.

Reaching for the binoculars Mop had given him, Alex scanned the horizon for a sign of a building, but all he could see were trees. Lots and lots of trees. One, however, towered above all the others. It was located at the far end of the lake—too far away to make out any details—but Alex had a hunch it was there that they'd find Tom.

"In a tree?" said Sarah, after Alex had shared his thoughts with her. "Are you mad? No one lives in a tree."

Alex shrugged. "I didn't say in a tree. But I have a hunch that's where we'll find him. Assuming, of course, this boat thing floats."

"I won't hold my breath," said Sarah.

But float it did, as Alex found out to his immense relief after they'd made the steep climb down to the lake. Once he'd inflated the boat, he dropped it in the water, placed what remained of their belongings in it, and helped Sarah climb aboard. Turning the bathtub-sized vessel around, he pushed it into deeper water and jumped in.

"Now this is sailing!" With one hand on the rudder and the other holding the umbrella-sail as it caught enough of a breeze to push them down the lake, Alex was becoming increasingly excited at the prospect of finally reaching the end of their journey.

"I wonder what kind of house Tom lives in?" asked Sarah.

"Probably log," said Alex.

"Better have hot running water."

Alex chuckled. "Somehow, I doubt it," he said, trying hard to stifle a yawn.

They travelled in silence down the middle of the lake for some time, enjoying their first breather since leaving Mop. After a few hours dozing on and off, it was Sarah who eventually spoke. "I think we're sinking," she said matter-of-factly, pointing to one of the boat's supposedly airtight compartments.

Using the small bellows, Alex quickly reinflated the boat-cloak. No sooner had he finished when a movement on the shoreline caught his eye. "Did you see that?" he said, pointing to a clearing on the far shore. "Something big jumped in the water."

"Please, Alex. I don't think I can handle any more surprises."

"There!" he exclaimed, pointing to a distant ripple in the water that grew steadily larger as it closed in on them. "Boy, it's fast! And big."

Alex caught a glimpse of a large shadow passing underneath the boat-cloak. Leaning over the side of the vessel for a better look, he scanned the water below for a sign of whatever it was that had swum toward them, but saw nothing. "This must be one deep lake."

Without warning, the boat suddenly rocked violently. Sarah screeched as she clung to its sides desperately. "What's happening?"

Before Alex could respond, he and Sarah were tipped into the lake. Scrambling quickly back on board, Alex panicked when he realized Sarah was nowhere to be seen. Catching a glimpse of colour a few feet below the water's surface, he swiftly pulled off his boots and shirt. Attaching a length of rope to his waist, he secured the other end to the boat and dove into the water, reaching Sarah before she could be swallowed up by the cold, dark depths of the lake.

Wrapping an arm around her, he used his free hand to pull himself upward as he kicked hard with his legs, thankful for the added buoyancy of the boat-cloak. Holding Sarah's head above water, he scrambled aboard then struggled to pull her limp body in after him. Flipping her onto her stomach, he placed her head on her hands. He then placed her head on her hands and pushed down on her back trying to force air into her lungs.

"Breathe, damn it, breathe!" he yelled desperately, his heart pounding as he continued his desperate attempt to revive her. After what seemed an eternity, Sarah's chest finally heaved as she coughed up water and gasped for air. Exhausted, but relieved, Alex slumped beside her, monitoring her breathing carefully until it returned to normal. Taking her cold hands in his, he rubbed them firmly until the warmth returned. Gently brushing her hair aside, he noticed a small gash on her temple.

Gazing down at Sarah, Alex had the strangest sensation that he, too, was being observed. Placing his shirt behind her head, he slowly reached into his backpack for the revolver. What he saw when he turned around was beyond anything he could have imagined.

As he watched, horror-stricken, a massive sea serpent rose slowly out of the lake, water pouring off its body like rain. Trembling with fear, Alex kept the gun pointed at the huge beast, even though he knew it would be useless against it. Keeping his finger on the trigger, he followed the movement of the serpent as it lowered its head toward him, stopping only when its enormous snout was no more than a few feet away. Bracing for the worst, he lifted the amulet from around his neck, hoping it would work its magic, just as it had done for Mop.

The serpent was now so close that Alex could have counted the coarse whiskers on either side of its nostrils. Its teeth—each as long as the sword he'd taken from the crypt—were set in double rows along its jaws like a shark's, and a crest of horns fanned out backwards from the top of its head like a giant spiky crown. Its skin was made up of countless overlapping scales similar to those of a snake. A scar stretched down its neck and along its torso, only ending where its bulky frame disappeared into the lake. Although much of its sleek, muddy-brown body remained submerged, Alex could see the silhouette of its enormous flat fins protruding like paddles from its sides. All the while, its tail swished back and forth in the water, as fidgety as that of a cat.

It was as if the serpent was studying him with its large, emerald green eyes. Yet he somehow sensed it wasn't interested in hurting him. Whether this was because of the amulet, he didn't know. But he realized it must have been watching him as he revived Sarah, quietly sizing up the strange little vessel and its two occupants, so tiny in comparison.

In spite of the danger—the serpent could easily have swallowed him in a single snap of its massive jaws—Alex felt something other than fear. It was the same sensation he experienced when comforting the Ultima dog, as if some ancient connection existed between them. Just what it all meant he had no idea, but the sense of peace it brought was strangely welcoming.

Without thinking, Alex lowered the amulet and placed a hand on the unexpectedly smooth skin of the serpent's snout. Almost imperceptibly, the scales beneath his hand slowly changed colour, the dull, dirty brown giving way to magnificent, almost luminous shades of gold, green, and blue. The serpent seemed to become agitated as a surge of energy shot up Alex's arm, jolting him like an electric shock.

Without warning, the serpent raised its massive head and let out a deep, booming roar that echoed across the lake, shocking Alex back into reality. The huge beast looked at him as if unsure quite what to make of the boy. Then, without warning, it lowered its head to Alex and snorted loudly, showering him in a spray of thick, sticky goo before turning and swimming swiftly away.

As soon as the serpent dove out of sight, a stunned Alex turned to Sarah to see if she'd witnessed the unusual encounter. To his dismay, she was still unconscious, completely oblivious of the incredible event that had just occurred. Dusk was drawing close, and he knew there was no hope of making it the rest of the way before nightfall. With Sarah uppermost on his mind, he steered toward shore to set up camp.

* * * * *

Alex sat mesmerized by the sparks dancing in the damp evening air hanging heavy over Wildeor, surrounded by a blanket of mist so thick he could barely see the shoreline just a few feet away. But he was worried. Sarah still hadn't regained consciousness, and he had no idea if his choice of campsite was safe. Although there was no sign of the serpent, every now and then he heard its distinctive call, as well as other strange noises, echoing eerily across the water. One of the strangest of these came from large bat-like creatures darting in and out of the treetops, their huge wings silently slicing through the night sky. With a high-pitched cry of *a-hool* they'd plunge into the lake after a fish. Despite the fact they kept their distance, Alex made sure the revolver and sword were close by, just in case.

After deflating and drying the boat-cloak, he wrapped it around Sarah like a blanket, tucking her in so snugly that all he could see in the fire's flickering light was the top of her flaming red hair. She looked like she'd been wrapped in a cocoon. Rubbing his bare arms briskly for warmth—he was cold after washing off the unpleasant goo the serpent had sprayed over him—he tossed more wood onto the fire. After hanging his shirt out to dry, he took stock of their remaining food supplies. All that was left were two tins of beans and some crackers buried in Sarah's backpack under a few items of clothing. Happy to have found something dry to wear—even if it was Sarah's—he wrapped one of her small sweaters around his shoulders like a cape.

Although exhausted, Alex fought hard to stay awake. He was determined to get Sarah to safety, even if it meant not sleeping. He also had a burning desire to find an answer to the one question that had bugged him since they'd fled Mortimer's Point: why me? The dramatic escape from the Ultima, his father's pocket watch, the letter from the Greystones, and Mrs. Pudsley's betrayal—what it all added up to, Alex didn't have a clue. But he was hopeful that Tom, when they finally found him, could set things straight.

It was then that Sarah began to stir, mumbling incoherently. Loosening the boat-cloak blanket, Alex placed a hand on her forehead. Although she was warm to the touch, Alex wouldn't be happy until she was back to her old self. Certain she'd be hungry, he used the sword to pierce the tops of the tins of beans, lifting off the lids and placing them on the edge of the fire. Sarah opened her eyes as they began to bubble.

"Welcome back," he said, barely able to conceal his relief.

"Wh . . . what happened," she asked softly as she sat up and shrugged off the boat-cloak. "Where are we?"

"Eat first," said Alex. Carefully pulling one of the cans out of the fire, he plopped in a spoon, crumbled a cracker into it and passed it to her. "Careful, it's hot."

Sarah wolfed the beans hungrily, the first hot food they'd eaten in days. "These are good!" she said, scraping the tin clean. "Any more?"

Alex passed her what was left of his.

"What happened back there?" she asked, tucking into the second helping of beans with gusto.

Alex didn't know where to begin. If he told the truth, she'd be too worried to let him rest—and he needed sleep. "What do you remember?" he finally asked.

"Nothing. Everything seemed calm and then . . . then I don't remember."

"You didn't see anything unusual?"

"Apart from you?"

Alex smiled, glad to see she hadn't lost her sense of humour. "It . . . it was a log," he said, thinking quickly. "Knocked us clean into the lake."

"A log," Sarah repeated, unable to hide her disbelief.

"That's right. You hit your head on it when you fell out. Next thing I knew, you were sinking. So I pulled you out and, well, I resuscitated you."

"Please tell me you didn't do anything gross like mouth-to-mouth?"

Alex's face reddened. "No, no. Of course not. It was something I learned from Red McPhee. He always said it might come in useful, working on the steamers and all."

"Was it him that said you should wear girls' clothes, too? Please don't make a habit of it, I've hardly got any left," said Sarah with a wry smile.

Alex watched anxiously as she stood up and walked unsteadily to the edge of the lake. "Can't see a thing," she said after rejoining him by the fire. "Where do you think this Tom guy's got to? He was supposed to meet us and—"

Sarah was interrupted by the loud, haunting call of the serpent echoing across the lake. Sarah squealed, grabbing Alex's arm so tightly it hurt. "What on earth was that?"

"I . . . I don't know," lied Alex.

After a few minutes of silence, Sarah finally let go of his arm. "Thanks for saving me."

"That's OK. You were in a pretty bad way."

Unexpectedly, Sarah leaned over and placed her arms around him, hugging him tightly. He stiffened like a plank. "I'm sorry I was mean to you when we first met," she said.

Letting go of him, she reached up and touched his hair, a quizzical expression on her face. "That's a different look. I like it. Not so slimy, nice and sticky-uppy. A little crunchy, perhaps." Sarah sniffed her fingers. "Smells a little strange, though. What is it?"

"Probably sap. Must have happened when I was collecting wood for the fire."

"You really are quite strange," said Sarah, reaching for the boat-cloak. "Why don't you get some sleep?" she said, shaking sand and leaves off the canvas material before throwing it over Alex's shoulders. "We can take turns keeping watch."

Alex didn't argue. Some shut-eye sounded like heaven. Covering himself with the boat-cloak, he lay on the ground, closed his eyes and quickly fell asleep.

He was dead to the world when Sarah suddenly shook him awake sometime later. "Get up," she whispered. "Something's out there!" She pointed in the direction of the lake as she hurriedly placed more wood on the nearly dead fire.

Alex sat up drowsily and peered into the swirling mist. "Probably just those big bats. Did it go *a-hool, a-hool*?"

Sarah looked at Alex like he was from another planet. "There was no noise, and this was no bat. It was in the water. More of a shadow, really. A big shadow. I dozed off. When I woke up, I felt like I wasn't alone."

"Probably just your imagination," muttered Alex. Handing Sarah the pistol, he told her not to use it unless absolutely necessary.

Sarah looked at the weapon for a few moments, then handed it back. "No bullets."

Checking the chamber, Alex was surprised to find she was right. Even if he'd wanted to use the gun against the serpent it would have proven useless. Casting it aside, he slunk back into the warmth of the boat-cloak.

"You've got your amulet," he said. "Animals don't like them."

"Why didn't it work on that cave monster, Wendy, or whatever it was called?"

"Another question for Tom. Now, can I please get some sleep?" Alex closed his eyes and rolled onto his side.

He was just dozing off again when Sarah pulled back the cloak and climbed in beside him. "Well, if we're going to be something's dinner, we might as well go together. And I'm cold."

Curling into a ball, Alex was mortified when Sarah pressed her back against his. "What are you doing? You're freezing!" he complained halfheartedly. Although uncomfortable with the situation, he knew she was right about keeping warm. "I guess it's OK," he mumbled sleepily. "So long as you don't snore."

Alex lay still for a few minutes, drifting in and out of sleep. "What on earth's that smell!" he suddenly exclaimed as he attempted to waft away the stench emanating from beneath the covers.

Sarah shook with laughter.

CHAPTER 8

UNEXPECTED GUESTS

"Boy? Boy! Wake up!" squealed the owner of the foot that kicked Alex painfully in the leg.

Springing to his feet, he came face to face with a man a few inches shorter than himself. The stranger was stooped and wizened, his face contorted with rage as he brandished his walking stick like a weapon. With his other hand, he clutched a long leash, which he jerked repeatedly.

As alarming as the unprovoked attack was the sight of the furry little animal at the end of the leash. About the size of a small child, with a thick coat of long, brownish hair and hands and feet like those of an ape, the creature was clearly frightened by the confrontation and stumbled over Sarah in its attempt to get away. Woken by the commotion, she screamed when the animal landed in her lap. Pushing it away in disgust, she scrambled to her feet. The animal seemed as upset as Sarah at their unexpected encounter.

"Blasted brute! Keep still!" shouted the peculiar little man, threatening the animal with his walking stick. Without thinking, Alex sprang forward and yanked the makeshift weapon from his grasp.

The rage in the stranger's eyes caused Alex to back away and adopt a defensive stance.

"Give that back at once!" shouted the stranger, specks of spittle shooting from his mouth as he tried to snatch back the walking stick. "Have you no tongue, boy? What are you doing here?"

Standing his ground, Alex studied the man intently. The stranger's pock-marked face was etched with deep creases, and his cold, coal-black, eyes darted back and forth between Alex and Sarah. His long nose curved downward, almost touching his upper lip, a drop of moisture clinging to its pointy end. His large yellow teeth protruded rat-like over his bottom lip. Despite the heat and humidity, he wore a tattered military overcoat and knee-length riding boots.

"Well?" the man demanded, his heavy accent unfamiliar as he wiped his constantly dripping nose on his sleeve. "What's your purpose here?"

Sarah joined Alex and, like him, stared defiantly at the man. "Never mind that, who are you?" she asked.

The stranger looked long and hard at the two dishevelled teenagers, a confused expression on his face. "Wait a minute . . . it can't be! You're Mortimer? But how did you get here?"

"You didn't know we were coming?" asked Sarah.

"Well, um, no, not exactly."

"If you're not Mr. Liat, then who are you?" asked Sarah impatiently.

The new arrival straightened up as much as his stooped back would allow. "I'm here in his place to welcome you in my official capacity as the Warden of Wildeor."

"Some welcome," mumbled Sarah.

"For that I apologize most humbly," said the warden, his demeanour changing as he adopted a more conciliatory attitude. "These are such difficult times. It's hard knowing just who one can trust."

"I know exactly what you mean," said Sarah, scornfully.

Alex was skeptical of the man's sudden attempt at sincerity. The pain from the blows he'd received still smarted, and he was unhappy with the warden's treatment of the defenceless creature now curled quivering in a ball in the dirt, whimpering pitifully.

"The name's Windlemore. Stanard Windlemore," said the weasely warden, motioning Alex to return the walking stick. "It's OK, boy. You can trust me."

Reluctantly, Alex handed it over.

"You could say I'm Tom's—Mr. Liat's—right-hand man," he continued, his mouth spreading in a wide, forced smile that only drew attention to his prominent stained teeth.

"More like Tom's thumb," muttered Sarah, just loud enough that the diminutive man might hear. "Where is Mr. Liat? We were told he'd help us . . . help me . . . find my parents. Can't you tell us what's going on?"

"All in good time," interrupted Windlemore, bowing slightly. "Now if you'll please gather your belongings, we really must press on. I'll take you to Mr. Liat's estate where you can rest and get cleaned up."

"We're walking?" asked Sarah. "Thank goodness! No more boats for me."

"I'm afraid I don't much like the water, either," said Windlemore with a sniff. Pulling a handkerchief from his coat, he blew his nose loudly. "Too unpredictable in these parts." Turning his attention back to the small animal, Windlemore yanked on the leash, dragging the unfortunate creature to its feet.

Alex stepped forward calmly and grabbed Windlemore's hand. Looking the man directly in the eyes, he asked him to stop. "Can't you see you're hurting it?"

As Windlemore relaxed his grip, Alex approached the animal, crouching down and extending a friendly hand. Obviously frightened due to Windlemore's harsh treatment, the animal cowered. Alex, however, persisted, and was soon able to scratch its head affectionately. As Alex stood up, the tiny creature wrapped its arms around his knees, holding Alex tightly, preventing him from walking away.

A surge of pity swept over Alex. That anyone could treat so defenceless an animal so cruelly was beyond comprehension. It was an unusual animal. Its rough, ruddy face and coarse skin were covered in soft, downy hair. It had a squashed nose and a wide lipless mouth, which opened to reveal snow white teeth, all flat except for four sharp incisors. Its thick hair was matted with the dirt of neglect, and it smelt almost as bad as Windlemore.

"There, little fellow, you're OK now," he said, beaming as he stooped to pick the creature up. "What on earth is it?"

"That," said Windlemore, "is a Sasquatch. Albeit a young one. Vicious, nasty creatures."

"Sorry . . . did you say Sasquatch?" asked Alex incredulously as he unfastened the tight chain from around its neck. "I thought they were just some terrifying myth. And gigantic, too!"

"All hype," said Windlemore, contemptuously, again blowing his nose noisily. "To keep people away."

Alex tipped out the meagre contents of his backpack, slid the Sasquatch in and placed it on his back.

"What, may I ask, do you think you're doing with the filthy thing?"

"I'm going to make sure you don't hurt it."

"They're parasites! Nothing but pestilence, full of dead skin, dust and other allergens. You're asking for trouble, Mortimer."

Alex cringed at Windlemore's tone. It reminded him of how Mrs. Pudsley would address him, a mix of contempt, anger, and bitterness.

"All such vermin must be dealt with," continued Windlemore. Vicious, evil creatures!"

"Surely Mr. Liat doesn't approve of your views?" asked Sarah.

"Ah, yes . . . Mr. Liat," said Windlemore, rubbing his hands together as a malicious grin spread across his face. "I'm afraid Mr. Liat is in no position to comment. He's . . . well, let's just say he's indisposed. As Warden of Wildeor, I'm taking care of his business."

"And what, exactly, does the Warden of Wildeor do? Apart from abuse animals," asked Sarah as she and Alex gathered up the rest of their belongings.

Windlemore smiled smugly, again wiping his nose on his sleeve. "I'm responsible for the wildlife here in Wildeor. And, alas, with Mr. Liat unavailable, it's on me that the great burden of running this godforsaken place has fallen."

"Doesn't sound like you're very happy with your work," said Sarah.

Windlemore ignored the comment. "Mr. Liat is, as you may or may not know, old. In fact, he's extremely old. He hasn't left his room, or even his bed, for months."

Helping Sarah with her backpack, Alex positioned himself so that Windlemore couldn't see him stash the revolver and sword amongst her belongings. They followed the surprisingly nimble man along a winding trail along the shoreline until, after about an hour, they reached a tree-lined canal at the end of the lake. Straddling the canal midway along its length was a large wooden gate. The first of anything manmade they'd seen since arriving in Wildeor, the structure resembled the kind of portcullis usually found at the entrance of a castle to keep intruders out.

Sensing Alex's curiosity, Windlemore offered an explanation. "Keeps those pesky brutes in Lake Idlerow where we can keep an eye on them."

Sarah turned to Alex with a puzzled expression on her face. Alex merely shrugged, pretending he didn't know what Windlemore was talking about. As they passed the gate and exited the forest, the enormous tree they'd seen from the other end of the lake came into view. Alex stopped dead in his tracks, awed by its size.

"Oh . . . my . . . God!" said Sarah. "That's impossible!"

Windlemore harrumphed in disgust. "It is indeed an abomination! A freak of nature, like everything else around here."

The tree was anything but freakish to Alex. Located on a hill in the middle of what appeared to be an island, it stood as tall as the waterfall they'd ducked through on their way to Wildeor, towering high above everything for miles around. Its huge branches— each as thick as a tree trunk—extended in every direction, its shadow stretching across the island.

"Now that's a tree!" Alex exclaimed.

"It's called Wid Dewr. The last of the giant golden oaks. Ghastly thing! It's where you'll stay while we decide what to do with you."

"In the tree?" asked Sarah, unable to hide her disapproval.

Windlemore smirked. "That's right. Shocking, isn't it?"

"It doesn't look very healthy," said Alex, pointing out the fact that many of the tree's leaves had begun turning brown.

"Oh, it's nothing," replied Windlemore dismissively. "Just a little dry, that's all. Not had much rain around these parts. Let's get a move on, shall we?"

From his vantage point, Alex could see that one of the trees on the near shore had a platform built about halfway up it, and was reached by a set of wooden stairs that wound their way around its trunk. Adjacent the platform, he could just make out what looked like an oversized wicker basket hanging from a rope stretching across the lake toward Wid Dewr. It was an aerial tramway with numerous other cables and ropes disappearing off in other directions.

Windlemore ushered them up the stairs, and once on the small platform, Alex was rewarded with an even better view of Wid Dewr. The island on which it stood was quite large, and was surrounded by the almost perfectly round moat-like lake. Much of the island had been planted with crops, including orchards of apples and peaches, as well as grains. He could also see a number of pastures fenced in with low hedges, and here and there small groups of as yet unidentifiable animals grazed. Clustered around the dock area were a number of barn-like structures and sheds, the largest of which stood two-storeys tall.

Windlemore opened the door to the cramped, roofless car of an aerial tramway and ushered Alex and Sarah inside. Once aboard, he squeezed in beside them, jostling for a position near a small set of levers. Trying not to glance downward, Alex clung tightly to Sarah as he tried not to squish the Sasquatch on his back. The car dropped sharply downwards as Windlemore pulled on the largest lever, causing Sarah to squeal at the unexpected lurching movement. Swaying from side to side like a pendulum, the car eventually settled as they began the slow journey to the opposite shore.

As they approached the next platform—this one located high up the trunk of a dead pine tree whose top had been lopped off—Alex was excited to see a small submarine tied to the dock below. Resembling an oversized fish, the submarine had the name *Argonaut* painted on its bow. Stacked higgledy-piggledy beside it were numerous wooden crates and cases, some opened to reveal weapons such as rifles and ammunition, as well as boxes of dynamite and barrels of gunpowder.

Before he could ask Windlemore the purpose of the cargo, the car jerked to a halt directly above the submarine. Alex leaned out for a better view. The length of a small yacht, it looked as if it could carry only a small crew. Alex was impressed with its sleek, old-fashioned beauty. The copper-covered wooden vessel had a small conning tower, and its three small chimneys were a clue to its surprising mode of power: steam.

Windlemore grabbed hold of another lever and off they set, only this time even slower as they began the ascent to Wid Dewr. As they approached, Alex was able to shuffle around enough to see that a doorway had been carved into its trunk a few feet above its base—a base so wide a house could have been hidden behind it. Curiously, many more doors, some with balconies, were positioned all the way up it, interspersed with the occasional window.

After a few more minutes travelling along the aerial tramway they bumped up against a large wooden platform hidden high up in the tree's dense foliage. Windlemore squeezed out of the car first and headed toward a doorway leading into the tree. Throwing the door open with a dramatic flourish, the warden turned and bowed to his guests.

"Welcome to Wid Dewr!"

CHAPTER 9

THE TREEHOUSE

The familiar scent of sap and sawdust greeted Alex and Sarah as Windlemore beckoned them into the treehouse. Holding open the door, he bowed slightly and offered a toothy grin. "Welcome to Wid Dewr." Closing the door behind him, he swiftly locked it before tucking the walking stick under his arm. "You never know what might want to get in," he said apologetically.

A small porthole-shaped window on the far side of the dark room provided just enough light to reveal a tattered rug on the floor, but little else. Opening a shoebox-sized control panel beside the door, Windlemore revealed an assortment of knobs and switches lined up in tidy columns. Despite the poor lighting, his hands moved nimbly as he tweaked and adjusted several of the controls then pressed a large black button in the middle of the display. An almost imperceptible hum followed, and a row of small, cobweb-covered light bulbs dangling from the ceiling began to flicker, bathing the room in a warm glow.

"Electricity!" said Sarah triumphantly. "I knew it!"

Windlemore closed the control panel, and for a brief moment seemed almost pleased. "Just one of our many upgrades. Powered by sap. Heaven knows we've got enough of it."

"Sap?" repeated Alex.

"Naturally. It's a hydrocarbon, like coal and gas. Burns exceptionally well." Windlemore pointed to a darkened corner where the walls were burnt to a charcoal finish. "Trees burn so very well once the sap ignites. Whoosh! Gone in seconds."

As the lights brightened, Alex could see the room served as the main entrance to the treehouse. Muddied work boots lay in a heap near a bench, and a coat rack stood guard next to the door, all but hidden under the weight of countless faded coats and musty furs. Beside it stood an umbrella stand with several walking sticks similar to the one Windlemore carried. Placing his walking stick in the stand, Windlemore shrugged off his overcoat and slung it onto the coat rack, sneezing uncontrollably. "Blasted dust! As if the pollen wasn't bad enough."

The room looked as if it had literally been whittled out of the tree. The interior walls were worn smooth, and here and there shiny patches of amber-coloured resin flickered in the dim light like tiny mirrors. Alex couldn't resist touching one such sticky patch.

"Such a nuisance," Windlemore said as he watched Alex. "Especially in spring. We tap as much as we can, but the wretched stuff's always leaking."

"Is that what those are for?" asked Sarah, pointing to a series of pipes running along the ceiling.

"No, that's the plumbing. The same system that generates electricity heats the water and pumps it around the tree. It also pumps nutrients."

"Surely trees get those from the soil?" asked Alex

Windlemore looked at Alex with disdain. "Gravity, Mortimer, prevents water and nutrients getting past a certain height. To keep this monstrosity alive, Mr. Liat had to give it a helping hand. Now, if you'll follow me, I'll take you to your rooms."

As Windlemore darted down a dark stairwell, Alex took a closer look at the hefty wooden door on the opposite side of the room. It had solid iron hinges and an ornate brass handle in the shape of a serpent's head. Alex wondered what secrets might lie behind it. His curiosity was aroused further by the fact the heavy bolts at the top and bottom of the door were drawn closed.

Shifting his attention back to Windlemore, he followed the small man down the tight, circular stairs, careful not to bang his head on the low ceiling. The room he entered was small and cluttered, the only furniture in it an old comfy chair, a couch, and a reading desk with a small portable stove, saucepan and kettle sitting on it. A four-poster bed, a bathtub and toilet were located in a small adjoining room separated only by an old curtain affixed to the ceiling. It looked as if it hadn't been occupied for quite some time.

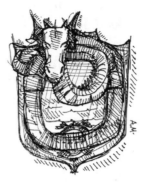

"These are your quarters," said Windlemore, banging the palm of his hand on the dusty couch. The small man let out a sneeze that shook his puny frame.

"It's not exactly private," complained Sarah.

"We've had far more illustrious guests than you visit us, and not one of them ever complained about the accommodations," said Windlemore, sniffing as he wiped his nose on his sleeve.

"Such as?" asked Sarah.

Windlemore picked up an old leather-bound book from the desk. Blowing off a cloud of dust, he sneezed again, this time all over the book. "Makes for an interesting read. Some very famous names. Although, perhaps, none as infamous as young Mortimer here."

With a look of disgust, Sarah took the book from Windlemore. "Sorry," he apologized. "Allergies, such a nuisance."

"What do you mean by infamous?" asked Alex.

"It's all a matter of perspective. But I must say how surprised I am that you know so little about your heritage, Mortimer. There are those who have waited many, many years to find you and—" Windlemore paused.

"And?" prompted Sarah.

"Let's just say there are some who would prefer that Mortimer and his like simply—how can I put this delicately—simply weren't around."

Alex frowned, unsettled by the direction the conversation was headed.

"May I ask which of those groups you belong to?" asked Sarah.

Windlemore stared long and hard at Alex before responding. "That, Miss Greystone, is for me to know and you to find out. In the meantime, do make yourselves comfortable. I'll find a change of clothes for you, and I dare say you'll want some food."

"When can we see Tom . . . I mean, Mr. Liat?" asked Alex.

"All in good time, Mortimer. You must rest, and I have urgent business to attend to. Your unexpected arrival requires some changes to our plans. In the meantime, I must ask that you remain here in your quarters. Now, if you'll excuse me—"

Windlemore hesitated as if suddenly remembering something. "Ah, yes, the creature. If you'd be so kind as to hand him over."

Alex shook his head. "No way. We'll keep him here with us until we've had a chance to speak with Mr. Liat."

Windlemore scowled at Alex, obviously displeased with the response. "As you wish," said Windlemore with a bow as he made for the stairs. "You may care for the wretched thing for the time being. Until then, I bid you adieu."

Once certain Windlemore had gone, Sarah shrugged off her backpack and dropped it to the floor. "That is one very nasty man! I can't believe we came all this way only to be met by such a creep!"

Alex carefully removed his backpack before reaching in and freeing the small Sasquatch. Leaping into his arms, the frightened creature quivered as it clung tightly to his neck.

"At least something around here likes you," said Sarah making her way to the tub. "I'm going to take a bath. I'm beat."

The Sasquatch still in his arms, Alex sat down on the old couch in the living area and instantly fell asleep.

* * * * *

"You awake yet?"

Alex didn't budge. He'd been dreaming of the serpent, and he didn't want it to end.

"We need to talk!" said Sarah insistently.

Eyes heavy with sleep, Alex tried—and failed—to stifle a yawn. "Go away." He was exhausted after the trek to Wildeor and the comfortable couch proved as welcoming as any bed. Waking up, as far as Alex was concerned, wasn't an option. "Let me sleep . . . I'm so tired."

Sarah, however, clearly had other ideas. Before Alex could protest, he was jolted awake by something being dropped in his lap. It was the guest book. "I think you should take a look at it."

Sarah had changed into the clothes Windlemore left for her and looked, thought Alex, like a farmer. Or a hillbilly. The denim dungarees were way too big, and the huge plaid shirt covered her like a tarp; her arms stuck through the baggy, but rolled-up sleeves, like two sticks. Most startling, however, was her hair—the long, red locks had been cropped short.

"What happened to you?" he asked.

Sarah blushed. "I've always wanted it short, but Mom wouldn't let me. But she's not here right now, is she?"

"It looks nice," said Alex. "Just a little different, that's all."

Sarah smiled coyly. "Just wait 'til you see Bogfoot! I gave him a bath. Boggy, here boy!" she called. The Sasquatch bounded into the room and jumped onto Alex's lap.

"Bogfoot? Boggy? What kind of names are those for a ferocious beast like this little fella? And what on earth is he wearing?" he asked, pointing to the underwear the Sasquatch had on.

Sarah chuckled as she described the Sasquatch's interest in the toilet. Convinced she could teach the animal some bathroom etiquette, she attempted to potty train him. But as she struggled to teach him to perch on the rim of the bowl, he slipped in, wedging one of his oversized feet in the bend.

"It took a while to get it out, poor guy. I thought of calling him Bigfoot at first, but that just seemed a little too obvious. Bogfoot has such a nice ring to it."

"And you said I was crazy! What about the, um, undies? A tad over the top, aren't they?"

Bogfoot, it seemed, felt no such shame regarding Sarah's crowning achievement in her Sasquatch-domestication program. Confessing that she was a little squeamish about the animal's boy bits, she fashioned a pair of underwear from one of the plaid shirts Windlemore had left for them. "Bogfoot's undies," she joked, as she leant forward and gave them a tug.

Alex took a whiff of the creature's clean thick coat, pleased it no longer smelt like skunk. Putting Bogfoot down, he next turned his attention to the book Sarah had given him. The first dozen or so entries were handwritten, with a short notation preceding each of them. It said: TRANSCRIBED FROM THE ORIGINALS CARVED INTO THE GOLDEN OAK, WID DEWR.

Still a little sleepy, Alex looked at Sarah for clarification. "I don't get it."

"Look at the dates! Those first few were all here before books even existed. Read some of them."

Alex did as instructed. "Leif Ericson. Who was he?"

"A Viking. Came to North America five hundred years before Columbus. Who, by the way, is also here. See?" Sarah pointed to an unrecognizable signature, beside which someone had printed: CHRISTOPHER COLUMBUS, 1493. Sarah told Alex to keep reading. "It gets better."

"George Washington," read Alex, flicking through the pages and calling out names randomly. "Abraham Lincoln. Charles Darwin. Mark Twain. This is a joke, right?"

"That's what I thought. Then I found this." Sarah took the book and flipped forward a few pages. Running her finger down the entries, she handed the book back to Alex after finding what she was searching for.

Alex nearly choked when he saw the words: COL. WALDEN, JAN. 01, 1901.

"That's the name on my watch!"

The rest of the entry read: WINTER IN WILDEOR IS A WONDROUS THING! THANK YOU, MORTY, FOR ENTRUSTING ME WITH THE TITLE OF LORD OF ALLEGIANCE. PROUD TO BE ONE OF THE FEW! YOUR FRIEND AND COMRADE, COL. W.

Alex let the book fall to his lap, unable to believe what he'd just read. "He's been here, Sarah! My dad's been here."

Sarah was equally excited. "Along with some of the most remarkable people in history. Some of the greatest thinkers and leaders of all time! They've all been here, Alex. Abraham Lincoln might have bathed in the same tub as me. Think of it!"

"I'm trying hard not to," responded Alex as he paced the room. "We have to make that weasel Windlemore tell us what's really going on. And we need to find Tom."

"Yes, but where is he?"

"We know he's in Wildeor somewhere. Windlemore's the key." Alex smacked his hand against his forehead. "That's it! Keys! We haven't seen Windlemore with any keys, yet somehow he manages to lock the doors. If we could only find out where he keeps them, we'll find Tom."

"And get out of this damn tree," said Sarah.

"Where is he anyway?" asked Alex.

"Down at the docks."

Picking up the binoculars, Alex stepped toward the small doorway located on the outer wall. He guessed the platform must have been at ground level at some point in time, and had moved higher and higher as the tree grew. He estimated the doorway was now situated about halfway up it. It had no balcony or steps, and all that prevented him from falling out were two wooden planks nailed across the opening and a helpful sign that simply said, MIND THE GAP.

From his lofty perch Alex could see Windlemore sorting through the dockside cargo, which he'd clearly been distributing amongst the various nearby buildings.

"For such a miniscule moron, he's pretty strong," commented Sarah. "What's he doing down there?"

"Moving crates of explosives. Though what they're for I haven't got a clue." Alex continued to watch as Windlemore closed the submarine's hatch. "Looks like he's finished for the day. Funny, he's never without that walking stick. Yet he doesn't seem to have any problems walking."

"They're mostly for decoration," said Sarah.

"He is a little old-fashioned. Let's take a look around before he gets back."

Alex made straight for Windlemore's collection of walking sticks. Picking one up, he could tell from its weight and feel that it was made of a hard wood, perhaps hickory or ash. The shaft, painted a rich cherry red, was dull with age and use. Where they differed was in the grip. The one he was holding was crowned with a skull carved out of ivory, its deep-set eyes containing two tiny red rubies that sparkled menacingly. Placing it back in the stand, he ran his hands along the row of walking sticks, fascinated by the diversity: a wolf's head, its fangs barred in a fierce growl; a wild boar, its sharp tusks made from tiny slivers of ivory; and an intricately carved eagle, clutching a snake in its sharp talons.

But the one that really caught Alex's attention had a serpent's head for a grip. Made of gold, where the others were silver, its scales were formed from glittering jewels including emeralds, rubies, and diamonds.

"What's so special about that one?" asked Sarah. "You look like you've seen it before."

"I . . . I think I have," said Alex as he gazed upon the grip in wonder.

"That's interesting," said Sarah. "It's just like the knocker on that door over there. And this one," she said, tapping the wolf's head, "is the same as the one on the door in our room."

The telltale sound of a key turning in a lock announced Windlemore's arrival. Alex quickly placed the walking stick back in the umbrella stand. Turning toward the guest quarters, they were spotted by Windlemore before making good their escape.

"What are you two up to?" he asked suspiciously, surveying the room. "I thought I told you to stay in your quarters!"

Alex quickly diffused the situation. "We . . . we wanted to ask you a few questions."

Alex couldn't help but notice that the warden turned his back on them when locking the door as if to hide what he as doing. Once done he put the walking stick away and threw his coat on the stand.

Leaning forward, Alex confirmed that the walking stick's handle matched that of the door Windlemore had just entered. The ferocious bears matched perfectly. Once relieved of his coat, Windlemore reached down and picked up the walking stick with the serpent's head.

"What sort of questions?" Windlemore asked.

"Like, why are you keeping us locked up?" asked Sarah.

"Locked up? Oh no, not at all! Simply a precaution to ensure nothing gets in."

"You mean gets out." said Sarah.

Windlemore could barely conceal the contempt on his face. "I'm quite sure I have no idea what you mean. Now, if you'll excuse me, it's late," he said, shepherding Alex and Sarah back to the guest rooms "I will retire to my quarters. I shall be heading out to Sawdust City for supplies in a day or two. There'll be plenty of time for you to explore later."

"We'll see Mr. Liat?" asked Alex.

"I shall confer with Mr. Liat on that very topic this evening and report back to you. I bid you goodnight." With that curt response, Windlemore slammed the door leading to the guest quarters and bolted it from the outside.

Sarah turned to Alex with an exasperated expression on her face. "He's not keeping anything out. He's keeping us in!"

CHAPTER 10

THE BEASTS OF WILDEOR

A lex was restless. Two days had passed since Windlemore's promise to take them to Tom, and yet the warden seemed to do his utmost to avoid them. By the time Alex got up each morning, Windlemore was already at the docks, or poking around the numerous buildings near the animal enclosures. And at the end of the day, he'd somehow sneak back into Wid Dewr unheard.

Fortunately, Bogfoot kept him occupied while he waited for something—anything—to happen. Playful as a pup, the energetic little Sasquatch quickly learned to follow a few basic commands, including how to fetch: all Alex had to do was point at something across the room and, quick as a flash, Bogfoot went and got it.

It was during one such trip that the Sasquatch retrieved a rather unusual book. The size of a city phone book, and as well thumbed, *Trackin' Jack's Compendium of Curious Critters* was a decade's old directory of bizarre creatures allegedly native to North America. Along with meticulous sketches and notes regarding the identification and tracking of animals like the Furry Three-toed Tree Toad, the book offered useful tips on such things as how to remove the poisonous quills from the fearsome Porcupike; how to skin a Lesser Spotted Mooseskink; and how to survive a Grizzled Wallamalloo attack (simply ignoring the large, overly sensitive anthropoid was apparently the best bet).

His curiosity aroused, Alex took a closer look at the contents of the bookshelf. Along with the usual collection of reference guides, encyclopedias and travelogues, were a handful of weird and wonderful titles similar to the one he'd been given by Bogfoot. Amongst them were such doorstoppers as Arnold Slackjaw's authoritative *Stuff That Really Matters: Answers to Everything That Ever Was, Is, and Is-Yet-to-Be* and *Altercations with a 500-Pound Man-Eating Turkey and Other Abominations* by Waldo "*Bushman*" Strap. But what most impressed Alex was a large old leather-bound book entitled *The Beasts of Wildeor*. Handwritten in a tidy, old-fashioned style, it turned out to be a comprehensive encyclopedia of the wildlife of the remarkable nature reserve Alex now found himself in.

Trackin' Jack's a Porcupine

It was to the section on sea serpents that Alex turned first:

SEA SERPENTS ARE CLOSELY RELATED TO THE LONG-EXTINCT LAND DRAGON, AND ARE WIDELY BELIEVED TO BE THE LAST REMAINING DRAGON SUBSPECIES. OFTEN REFERRED TO AS SEA DRAGONS, SEA SERPENTS USUALLY HAVE LONG, BENDY BODIES. ALTHOUGH THEIR NUMBERS HAVE BEEN GREATLY REDUCED, SMALL NUMBERS CAN STILL BE FOUND IN REMOTE LOCATIONS SUCH AS WILDEOR.

SEA SERPENTS COME IN MANY SHAPES, SIZES, AND COLOURS, ALTHOUGH BLACK, BROWN, AND GRAY ARE MOST COMMON. SOME OF THE RAREST AND MOST EXOTIC VARIANTS CAN CHANGE COLOUR DEPEND-

ING UPON THEIR MOOD OR, IN THE CASE OF THE HIGHLY EVOLVED WILDEORIAN SEA DRAGON, WHEN HANDLED BY THEIR KINDRED SPIRIT (NOTE: SEE WILDEORIAN SEA DRAGON, PAGE 1535).

Turning eagerly to page 1535, Alex was rewarded with a colourful illustration of the creature he'd seen days earlier, along with the following additional details:

THE WILDEORIAN SEA DRAGON IS UNIQUE DUE TO ITS ABILITY TO CHANGE COLOUR WHEN INTERACTING WITH ITS KINDRED SPIRIT. AT SUCH TIMES, ITS DULL, MUDDY BROWN SKIN, MADE UP OF LARGE OVERLAPPING SCALES LIKE A SNAKE, TRANSFORMS INTO A VIBRANT DISPLAY OF COLOURS, WHICH SHIMMERS DIAMOND-LIKE FOR MANY HOURS. ADULT WILDEORIAN SEA DRAGONS CAN GROW HUNDREDS OF FEET IN LENGTH, AND MOVE IN A ROLLING, UP-AND-DOWN MOTION, PROPELLING THEMSELVES USING THEIR LONG TAILS AND A PAIR OF PADDLES LOCATED ALONG THEIR TORSO. THEY MAY, ON OCCASION, DISPLAY A HUMP ABOVE WATER (PARTICULARLY WHEN ANGRY).

THE WILDEORIAN SEA DRAGON HAS A HEAD SHAPED LIKE THAT OF A HORSE AND HAS LARGE, CATLIKE EYES (USUALLY GREEN, BUT SOMETIMES BLUE OR YELLOW). A SET OF COARSE WHISKERS—CRUCIAL FOR NAVIGATION IN DEEP, DARK UNDERWATER LOCATIONS—IS ATTACHED TO ITS SNOUT EITHER SIDE OF ITS NOSTRILS. ITS LONG, SHARP TEETH ARE SET IN DOUBLE ROWS ALONG ITS JAWS. ATOP ITS HEAD SITS A CREST OF HORNS, LIKE A CROWN. IT NO LONGER HAS ANY NATURAL ENEMIES, ALTHOUGH IT CAN BE HARMED OR EVEN KILLED BY HUMAN OR OTHER INTERVENTION, EITHER BY ACCIDENT OR DELIBERATELY. THE WILDEORIAN SEA DRAGON HAS BEEN INTRODUCED TO HABITATS IN EUROPE, ASIA, AND NORTH AMERICA WITH VARYING DEGREES OF SUCCESS.

Skipping past the material regarding the serpent's diet and other mundane topics, Alex was fascinated by the last few lines of the entry. He read them over and over to ensure he fully grasped their meaning:

WITH AN AVERAGE LIFESPAN EQUAL TO THAT OF ITS KINDRED SPIRIT, WILDEORIAN SEA DRAGONS HAVE BEEN RECORDED TO LIVE

WELL OVER 500 YEARS. IN ORDER TO REACH SUCH AN AGE, IT MUST FIRST HAVE BONDED WITH ITS KINDRED SPIRIT WITHIN THE FIRST YEARS OF LIFE, AND THE BOND MUST REMAIN UNBROKEN.

Could he be the Kindred Spirit of the serpent, or sea dragon, he'd encountered? It did, after all, respond to his touch. But regardless of the evidence, he couldn't bring himself to believe that he would ever be considered worthy of so such a title.

Browsing through the book as he considered these possibilities, Alex stumbled across a diagram of the horrible monster that had chased them through the mountain. It was called a Wendigo.

"I think I found Wendy," said Alex, summoning Sarah to inspect the picture. Here's what the book said:

THE CANNIBALISTIC WENDIGO IS A SOULLESS, EVIL, INSATIABLE HUMAN-LIKE CREATURE. NEVER SATISFIED WITH KILLING AND CON-SUMING JUST ONE INDIVIDUAL, IT CONSTANTLY CRAVES NEW HUMAN VICTIMS. MANY TIMES LARGER THAN A HUMAN, THIS VILE, REPULSIVE CREATURE GROWS IN PROPORTION TO THE MEAL EATEN AND IS PER-PETUALLY HUNGRY. AVOID AT ALL COSTS!

"Sounds like some of the old hags at school," remarked Sarah drily.

Alex laughed. Delving deeper into the book, he noticed the names of some animals had been crossed out, with the word Mortuus scrib-bled over them, along with a date.

"What does Mortuus mean?" he asked.

"Sounds Latin. I think it means dead, or extinct."

Alex showed Sarah some of the entries containing the word. In the w's alone, these included the Waheela, a bear-dog; the Wulver, a wolf-man; and the Wani, a dragon-like crocodile.

"What's it say about our little Sasquatch?" asked Sarah.

Flipping to the relevant entry, Alex was horrified to see that it, too, had the word Mortuus scribbled across it. But it was the date that sur-prised him: August 10, 1929—the current year. "What's the date to-day?"

"Let me see . . . I was shanghaied by Mop July thirtieth," said Sarah.

"So today must be . . . yes, August sixth, I think. Why?"

Alex showed Sarah the date in the book. "That's strange," she said. "How could anyone know when a creature is to become extinct?"

"They would if they were the ones doing it."

Sarah was clearly shocked. "Do you think it's Windlemore?"

Alex picked up the Sasquatch, hugging him tightly. "He sure doesn't like animals very much. Especially this little guy. And sea—" Alex caught himself before letting slip his encounter with the sea dragon.

"And what?" asked Sarah.

Alex fumbled for words. "And . . . and, um, nothing, really."

"Alex, you're acting kind of odd. Even for you."

"I can't help feeling something just isn't right," he said in an attempt to steer the conversation in a different direction.

"You mean Windlemore?"

"It's not just him. Something inside me feels . . . I don't know . . . uneasy. I get this feeling something bad's about to happen."

"That's a cheery thought. You better not be going anywhere. Not yet, anyway. And certainly not unless I've got something to do with it."

While Sarah continued playing with Bogfoot, Alex spent the rest of the day poring through *The Beasts of Wildeor*. He was fascinated by the tremendous variety of creatures that called this extraordinary wilderness home—or once did—and was still immersed in his reading when he heard a door closing in the main hallway. It was followed immediately by the thumping of feet as Sarah ran to intercept Windlemore.

"Hey!" she hollered, pounding her fists against the door. "Let us out! Do you hear me, Windlemore?"

Alex's heart sank when, seconds later, another door was heard closing. Windlemore clearly had no intention of letting them out. He realized it was up to them to do something to change the situation, and soon.

"I'm zonked," said Sarah despondently, turning down her bed. "We've got to do something about that sneaky good-for-nothing bum! I just know he's up to no good," she added as she climbed into bed. Bogfoot curled up beside her.

"I hear you," said Alex, deep in thought. "You get some rest. We'll work on a plan tomorrow."

Alex didn't let on that a very different plan was beginning to take shape in his overactive mind.

Chapter 11

THE SEA DRAGONS

Getting out of the big tree was a lot easier than Alex had expected. Aided by the light of the full moon and the tree's dense foliage, he was able to rappel by rope down to a rickety balcony adjacent one of the many doorways that were dotted along the length of the tree. From it, a long-abandoned rope footbridge descended toward the cluster of buildings near the docks. Although the rope was frayed and many of the wood boards were rotten, the footbridge promised the most direct route down to the water.

Testing each board cautiously, Alex made his way slowly along the swaying bridge, his heart skipping a beat every time it creaked or cracked. He was soon standing on the roof of one of the larger dock-side buildings, and after climbing down a rope ladder he found himself on solid ground for the first time in days. But his relief was short-lived. From out of nowhere a flock of what he first thought were sheep surrounded him, shuffling and bumping against him in their eagerness to find food. But there was something distinctly different about these sheep.

Before leaving, he'd packed a number of items into his backpack that he thought might prove useful during his little adventure, including a flashlight, *The Beasts of Wildeor*, and a loaf of bread as a treat for the sea dragon. Pulling out the bread to distract the animals now surrounding him, he was practically stampeded as they grunted and snuffled greedily. Upon closer inspection, he was puzzled to see the sheep were in fact pigs—woolly pigs. Tossing the loaf into the field as a distraction, Alex hopped over a gate into an adjoining field to escape the comical-looking hogs. To his dismay, the field, too, was home to more equally strange creatures. He now stood in the midst of a flock of noisy, knee-high, flightless birds that looked strangely familiar in the moonlight. To his complete surprise, he recognized them almost immediately: Dodos!

As he reached out to stroke one of the overfriendly birds, a light in the treehouse suddenly turned on. Throwing himself into a hedge for cover, Alex peeked out to see Windlemore silhouetted against one of the upper windows, obviously woken by the noise of the animals. Fortunately, the cackling of the Dodos and the grunting of the woolly pigs soon died down, and the light in the treehouse was extinguished. Peace once again settled upon Wildeor.

Hauling himself out of the hedge, Alex picked his way carefully through the ramshackle collection of barns and sheds. As he neared the largest building, a familiar clucking sound led him to believe he'd stumbled across a chicken coop. He wasted no time opening the large creaky door, excited about the prospect of supplementing the almost inedible stew Windlemore had been feeding them with a few fresh eggs. The moment he entered the pitch-black building, however, the animal noises stopped, replaced by an unsettling silence.

Alex unlatched the door of the closest pen and entered cautiously. At the back of the empty straw-lined coop sat a nest as big as a bathtub.

He was astounded to find in it an egg the size, shape and colour of a watermelon. As he picked it up and tucked it under his left arm, he felt a strange tickling sensation on his neck. Reaching behind, Alex was startled to feel his hand brush against something soft and feathery.

Shining his flashlight upward, he was horrified to see the tickling came from a cluster of feathers attached to a long, thin tail. But it was what lay at the other end of the tail that caused the most alarm. The size of a man, the giant bird had the head of a rooster and a thick beak that looked strong enough to shatter wood—or bone. Stubby wings, too short to be of use for anything but balance, protruded from its sleek, reptilian body. Three talon-tipped toes, each curved and dagger-deadly, enabled it to cling to its perch.

Petrified, Alex backed slowly toward the door, hoping that the monstrous bird hadn't seen him picking up the egg. But as he looked up again, he could see its cold, jet-black eyes staring directly at him, watching his every move intently before dropping clumsily from its perch onto the floor. Tucking the egg under his arm like a football, Alex wrenched open the stall door and ran for the building's exit. But he tripped in his haste to get away, and the bizarre bird quickly caught up with him, looming over him menacingly as he lay helpless on the ground.

Alex instinctively kicked at the bird, sending it staggering backward, squawking angrily. Rolling quickly from under it, and still clutching the egg, he ran as fast as his legs would carry him to the door. But the bird jammed its huge beak in the doorway before he could pull it shut. He shoved hard against the door, causing the bird to emit a shrill screech as it pulled its head out of the way. Quickly bolting the door, Alex slumped to the ground to catch his breath.

It was only then that he noticed the sign on the door he'd just fought so hard to close: CAUTION! CRACOTILE BREEDING IN PROGRESS. ENTER WITH CAUTION. EXIT IF YOU CAN!

Although a little remorseful at having stolen the bird's egg, Alex felt no immediate desire to return it—at least, not until the bird was once again locked up safely. Brushing himself off, he found one of the Cracotile's tail feathers stuck in his boot. Placing it and the egg in his backpack, he turned once more toward the docks.

Only a small shed now stood between him and the waterfront. Making his way around it, he caught a glimpse of something familiar through the building's one tiny window. Pressing his face against the glass, Alex gasped in horror as he recognized the mummified remains of a Sasquatch propped up against a wall. Worse still was the grisly discovery of numerous Sasquatch hides piled high beside it, and three small, lifeless bodies dangling from hooks in the ceiling. Sickened by the awful sight, Alex's stomach heaved as he threw up beside the building. It was clear he'd stumbled across the truth behind Windlemore's refusal to let them out of the treehouse: the so-called Warden of Wildeor was exterminating the beasts in his care. The discovery strengthened Alex's resolve to escape and find Tom, even if it meant taking matters into his own hands. He knew he'd also have to tell Sarah about his discovery, and about the sea dragon.

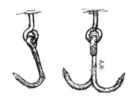

Regaining his composure, Alex inflated the boat-cloak and paddled swiftly and quietly to the far shore of the moat. Portaging past the canal gate, he was soon back in the water and paddling across Lake Idlerow, stopping now and then to shine his flashlight in wide arcs or to occasionally slap the water with then oar in the hope of attracting the sea dragon's attention.

After an hour of fruitless searching he was distracted by a ghostly light floating toward him across the lake. He watched enchanted as the balloon-sized apparition was joined by others, all of them circling slowly around the boat. Touching the one closest to him, Alex experienced the same tingling sensation that he'd felt when placing a hand on the sea dragon. In a flash of inspiration, he grabbed a piece of string from his backpack and carefully wound it around the unusual ball of energy and attached it to the boat. Soon a dozen shimmering lights were bobbing around him, buffeted by the gentle breeze, providing enough illumination to read by.

Reaching into his backpack for *The Beasts of Wildeor*, Alex searched for information regarding the ghostly lights. Here's what he found:

The Will-o'-the-wisp is the residue left behind after a soul has departed to the afterlife. It is thought to be the soul's outer skin. Only ever seen after nightfall, Will-o'-the-wisps drift across the earth, guided by the wind, discernable to only a few living souls. They shine brightly for many years after the soul has departed, gradually fading away until the light is extinguished for all eternity. (Note: See Corpse Candles.)

The Corpse Candles entry revealed the following additional information:

The Corpse Candle (or Ghost Candle) is the residue left behind after a Dark Soul has departed to the afterlife. It is thought to be the soul's outer skin. Darker than the blackest of nights, the Corpse Candles are a heavy, negative force as a result of carrying the burden of a Dark Soul. They tend to be found in dark places, such as swamps, caves, dungeons, etc. They have a tendency to adhere to those whose souls are already heavy, giving these living beings a look of world-weariness, as if they carry great burdens (they do).

Alex was about to hunt for the reference to Dark Souls when he sensed he was being watched. His heart skipped a beat as he looked up from the book and saw the sea dragon, its head level with the boat-cloak, its body and much of its neck still submerged. Alex marvelled at the intelligence in its eyes as it took in the scene, its expression almost quizzical as it watched the Will-o'-the-wisps. It snorted at them playfully, causing the dancing lights to bob about wildly.

Unexpectedly, the sea dragon moved its snout so close Alex could feel its warm, watery breath. Placing his hand on the beast's snout, a jolt of electric energy shot through him. Time stood still as a series of dramatic images flashed through his mind, one after another, in quick succession. He saw deep oceans, other unusual creatures, explosions, a sinking ship, a sea of bodies, a lifeboat, a submarine—all images that seemed to be embedded in the beast's memory. It was as if the sea dragon somehow wanted to communicate these recollections to him, though he couldn't understand why.

Coming to with a start, Alex opened his eyes and gazed at the sea dragon in wonder. "What are you trying to tell me?" he said as the beast nuzzled against him. As before, the sea dragon's skin changed colour, the dirty brown replaced with magnificent, glowing shades of gold, green, and blue. This time, however, Alex kept his hand on the huge beast as it pressed against him, savouring the bond between them as the colours—as bright and as vibrant as stained glass windows— shot down the beast's thick neck until they covered its entire body.

The moment seemed to last an eternity. Alex had never before felt so alive, so alert, or so happy. The sea dragon seemed to share his emotions; although it defied logic, Alex knew his fate was somehow wrapped up with that of this magnificent creature.

Out of the corner of his eye Alex noticed another large shape approaching. It was another serpent. Smaller than his sea dragon—he'd already begun thinking of the beast as his own—this one seemed shy and kept its distance. Restless and playful, it pestered the larger sea dragon, which eventually tired of its behaviour and chased it away. Turning back to Alex, it snorted at him, spraying him with the same sticky snot-like substance as before. Alex gasped as the warm fluid struck him, as much in shock as disgust. The sea dragon then turned and swam after its friend, its brightly coloured hide slowly disappearing as it dove out of sight.

Thrilled to have seen the sea dragons, Alex did his best to wash the gloop off his face before releasing the Will-o'-the-wisps. It was time to return to the treehouse before Windlemore noticed he was missing— and time to tell Sarah about the sea dragons.

CHAPTER 12

THE DEATH MASKS

Sarah sat on the old couch, holding the large Cracotile egg as she contemplated what Alex had just told her.

"A week ago I'd have said you were insane," she said quietly as she passed the large egg back to him. "But in light of everything we've been through, maybe you're not so crazy after all."

Alex placed the egg under the desk and draped a towel over it. He knew he'd have to return it to its mother at some point, but for now, his focus was on Sarah. He'd dreaded having to tell her of his Sasquatch discovery, not to mention the sea dragon and the truth regarding her near drowning. He felt tremendous relief now the truth was finally out.

"How could anyone be so heartless?" Sarah asked, cradling Bogfoot protectively. "I know animals can be icky, but they have feelings, too."

"Exactly!" said Alex. "Which is why we have to stop Windlemore before it's too late. If it isn't already."

Sarah sighed. "There must be something we can do? If only we knew how he gets in and out of the tree. I've never seen him with a key. Only those stupid walking sticks."

"That's it! The walking sticks!" exclaimed Alex. It was like a light bulb had just been switched on. "I wondered why he always has a different one with him. I bet they're keys."

Sarah looked at Alex as if he'd lost his marbles.

"Think about it!" he continued. "Each walking stick matches one of the doors in Wid Dewr. And he's locked us out of the room he stores them in because he knows we don't trust him."

"We can't do much cooped up in here," said Sarah. "We need to figure out how to open that door leading to the top of the tree. That's where we'll find Tom."

Without any further prompting, Alex opened his notebook and began drafting a plan of action. He knew it was a long shot, but doing something was better than doing nothing. All that was needed was an unsuspecting Windlemore, and a lot of luck.

* * * * *

Alex woke early after a fitful sleep, more determined than ever to find Tom. Springing into action the moment he heard Windlemore enter the hallway, he pounded on the door as hard as he could. A surge of excitement coursed through his body when he heard the warden unlock the door.

"Pull yourself together, Mortimer!" said Windlemore, his face red with anger. "Whatever's the matter?"

"It's Sarah! I . . . I think she's dying!"

Pushing Alex aside, Windlemore vaulted down the stairs where Alex knew he'd find Sarah sprawled on the floor by her bed. With Windlemore out of the way, he hurried to the neatly lined-up walking sticks, grabbed the one with the serpent's head and twisted its grip firmly. After a few turns he was relieved to pull out an intricately cut key. It fit the door leading to the top of the treehouse perfectly. He twisted his wrist sharply, and heard a metallic click as he unlocked the door. Replacing the key, Alex put the walking stick back and swiftly unlatched the room's one small window. Sprinting back to the guest quarters, he arrived in time to find Windlemore depositing Sarah onto the bed.

"Stupid boy!" said the warden as he placed a blanket over Sarah.

"She's no more dead than you or I! Although," he puffed, "she's every bit as heavy." Pulling a small container from his coat, Windlemore dropped a pinch of snuff under her nose. Sarah inhaled sharply, then sneezed.

"Wh . . . where am I?" she muttered, clutching the blanket tightly to her chest. "What happened?"

"You fainted. Nothing serious, despite Mortimer's theatrics. To be on the safe side, however, make sure you get plenty of rest while I'm away."

"Where are you going?" Alex asked as innocently as possible.

"Supplies. There's a logging town on the other side of the mountains. Sawdust City. I'll take the *Argonaut*. It's a day or so travel."

"But we're on a lake," said Alex.

"Not your concern, Mortimer," said Windlemore dismissively. "I've prepared enough food to last you until my return. Now, if you'll excuse me, I must be off."

Sarah jumped out of bed the moment Windlemore locked and bolted the guest room door behind him. "Can you believe he said I was fat?"

Alex laughed, relieved that their plan seemed to be working. "He said you were heavy."

"There's a difference?" said Sarah, throwing off the blanket and snatching her clothes from the floor. "Look the other way, please. And find out where that horrid man has got to. There's no time to waste!"

Binoculars in hand, Alex looked out in time to see Windlemore climb from the aerial tramway and make his way to the submarine. "It's going to take him a couple of hours to build up enough steam to leave."

"That thing's steam? And a submarine?" said Sarah in disbelief. "Sounds like a recipe for disaster. So, are you ready?"

Alex needed no further prompting. Fastening a length of rope to the barrier across the outer doorway and tying the other end around his waist as he'd done the previous night, he cautiously felt his way around the wide tree. The thick, coarse bark was perfect for climbing, and in no time he found himself at the small window. Pushing it open, he wiggled his way through it, falling in a heap on the floor. Quickly back on his feet, he unlocked the guest room door.

Brushing past him, Sarah made her way to the small control panel by the doorway. "Just as I thought. See that?" she said, pointing at a clear pipe running along the ceiling. "Nothing in it, right? Windlemore's been starving the tree! He's trying to kill it. That's why the leaves are turning brown."

Peering into the panel, Sarah read off the labels for the switches. "Hot water. Cold water . . . huh, fire water? Aha! Here it is! Tree water. There, that should do it," she said, flicking the switch. Moments later a yellowish-brown liquid could be seen shooting along the pipe.

"How'd you know?" said Alex, impressed.

Sarah smiled modestly. "You're not the only one who's been spending time trying to figure out how this place works."

Windlemore, as suspected, had removed the walking sticks. But that didn't matter now as Alex focused his attention on the heavy door he'd unlocked earlier. Turning the handle, he tried to push it open. Nothing happened. Placing his shoulder against it, he shoved as hard as he could. The door still didn't budge.

"Are you sure you unlocked it?"

Alex was adamant. "Of course I did! Must be stuck."

Brushing Alex aside, Sarah pulled the door open effortlessly. "Pull, don't push," she said smugly. "Brains over brawn."

Entering the narrow stairwell, Alex was met by an overwhelming stale smell that reminded him of the damp below-deck odour of a steamship. Pressing on, he followed the steep stairs upward, eventually finding himself—with Sarah and Bogfoot close behind—standing in a cluttered room crammed with enough antiquities to fill a museum.

Along one wall, row upon row of dusty shelves were stacked with neatly labelled fossils, bones, and specimen jars. Picking up one of the larger glass containers, he examined the murky preservative and saw a large centipede-like insect, coiled as tight as a spring, its tiny head resembling that of an ape. A larger jar held a revolting bug the size of a rat. Four crab-like claws, razor sharp and deadly, jutted from its sides, and a serrated stinger as long as his index finger protruded from its rear end. But what most disturbed him were its cold, unearthly eyes. Turning the bottle around, Alex studied the faded writing on the label.

"Isle of Aslintas," he read. "It's a . . . a Makárôn, whatever that is."

Placing the jar back on the shelf, Alex picked up another. Floating in it was a miniature of his sea dragon. It had the same crest at the top of its head, the same long neck and body.

"You look like you've seen a ghost," said Sarah.

"It looks just like a sea dragon," said Alex, turning the jar to read the label. It said: WYRMAS OND WILDEOR, CAMBRIA.

A squeal from Bogfoot drew their attention. Playing boisterously in the packing material inside one of a dozen crates along the far side of the room, the Sasquatch tossed wood shavings into the air like confetti at a wedding, all the while shrieking like a child.

Pulling the rambunctious animal from the crate, Alex tried to calm him as he pried a plaster cast of a man's face from its hands. The mask bore an air of serenity, eyes closed as if sleeping. Turning it over, he found the name HERACLES, along with the date 3220 BC.

"Sounds like Hercules," commented Sarah. "Any other famous names in there?"

Placing the mask carefully back in the crate and placing Bogfoot on the floor, Alex pulled out another.

"Oh, that's an easy one!" said Sarah. "Shakespeare!"

Alex turned over the unmistakable image, complete with the playwright's trademark moustache and pointy beard. WILLIAM SHAKE-SPEARE, 1616 AD, was etched on the back of it.

Sarah reached into the crate and picked a mask. "Hey, I wonder if this is a relative of yours? Check it out," she said, passing it to Alex.

A chill ran down his spine when he saw the name LOUIS DE MORTEMER, LISORS, 1066. "Probably just a coincidence," he muttered. "And anyway, it's spelt wrong."

Alex removed another mask from the crate. It said RANULPH DE MORTIMER, WIGMORE, 1137. Another bore the name ROGER DE MORTIMER, 3RD BARON MORTIMER, 1330. Still another read GRAHAM MORTIMER, MORTIMER'S CROSS, 1889. To Alex's surprise, each spelling of the last name was the same as his.

"There's certainly a family resemblance," said Sarah. "Wait a minute . . . Mortimer's Cross. I've seen that name before." Sarah pulled her parent's notebook from the waistband of her jeans and quickly found the page she was looking for. "Here it is."

She passed the notebook to Alex. "Says here Graham Mortimer died under suspicious circumstances," he said. "His body was found at Mortimer's Cross in England. The same symbols discovered on the cross were found carved across his chest. A skull and crossbones engulfed in fire."

Alex passed the notebook back to Sarah, alarmed by what he'd read. Although thrilled to have stumbled across so many clues regarding his distant ancestors, he was desperate to find out more about his parents. Flipping through the mask collection the way you'd skim through a row of books in a library, he pulled one out every now and then to read its name.

"What are you looking for?" asked Sarah.

"I thought I might find my father. All these Mortimers—"

Sarah placed a hand gently on his shoulder. "I'm sure there's a good reason why he's not here. But we really should keep looking for Tom."

Alex sighed. "You're probably right. We can look at the rest of these later. If Tom's alive, he's got to be here somewhere."

"If he's dead he might be here somewhere," responded Sarah glumly as she continued exploring the cluttered room. "Wow! Take a look at this!" she said excitedly.

Alex joined her in front of a large tapestry that stretched from floor to ceiling along one side of the room. "This is really, really spooky," she said. "It's Stonehenge. Father took me there last year. Looks nothing like I remember it, though."

The scene was one of chaos. Many of the massive stones were splattered with blood, and the headless carcass of a large animal occupied the middle of the stone circle, its red and gold hide pierced by countless arrows and spears. Standing over it, a huge dragon, black as pitch, blood trickling from its mouth, fed upon the body.

Alex quickly realized the scene depicted a massacre. Terrified civilians were being pursued by a group of heavily armoured warriors, some on horseback, others riding strange winged lions with eagles' heads. Here and there amidst the carnage were some of the peculiar creatures Alex recognized from *The Beasts of Wildeor*.

Sarah tugged Alex's arm. "Come on, let's keep looking! We can come back later," she said.

Also eager to find Tom, Alex pulled himself away from the tapestry. Searching for a way up the tree, he examined the uneven interior walls carefully for a sign of a door. To his surprise, he found a lever tucked behind a corner of the tapestry. He pulled it forward and a small, concealed doorway opened in the wall in front of him.

Without any hesitation, Alex bounded up the steps, which led into a small, but well-stocked, kitchen. Surrounded by scorch marks, an oven had been built into the side of the tree adjacent a pantry, chock-a-block with tinned food, fruit, and vegetables.

Sarah ran her finger along the dark burn marks, showing the sooty residue to Alex. "I can't believe they haven't burned this place down," she said.

Their next stop was higher still up the tall tree. Unlike the rooms they'd been in so far, the library was bright and well lit, with numerous small windows lining its exterior walls. The room's only furniture was a heavy wooden chair resembling a throne; its many dusty bookshelves were crammed with books.

Sarah looked like a kid in a candy store. "It smells of learning!" she said breathlessly.

"Smells like old dogs," countered Alex. "Keep going, there'll be plenty of time to read later."

Another short climb led to a tiny room with a sign above its door that said Apothecary. A quick peek revealed a medical supply room the size of a broom closet. Bottles of all shapes and sizes crowded the shelves, and a small marble counter was cluttered with mixing bowls, mortars and pestles. A number of syringes, some unused, others containing traces of a blue tincture, lay scattered about haphazardly, along with a number of empty bottles.

Sarah picked up one of the bottles. "Arsenic! I hope we're not too late."

"You think Windlemore's been poisoning someone? Maybe Tom?" asked Alex.

"Let's not wait to find out!" said Sarah, pushing Alex up the narrow staircase.

The next door they came to had the name STANARD WINDLEMORE, WARDEN, painted across it. Underneath, the words PRIVATE! KEEP OUT had been added.

"That's one piece of advice I'll definitely pay attention to," said Sarah.

Continuing swiftly up the stairs, Alex soon found what he was looking for. Directly in front of him was a small door with the name Tom W. Liat engraved on it in large gothic lettering.

Alex turned to Sarah. "You ready?"

Sarah nodded. His heart pounding, Alex nervously pushed opened the door.

CHAPTER 13

THE OLD MAN WHO LIVED IN A TREE

Alex was stunned by what he saw as he entered the tiny bedroom. Tom W. Liat looked like a corpse. A very old corpse.

"We're too late!" cried Sarah. "Oh, the poor man! How could anyone do such a thing?"

Something, however, told Alex that Tom wasn't dead. At least not yet. Placing a hand on the old man's chest, he felt it rise and fall almost imperceptibly as he breathed. "He's alive!" exclaimed Alex, barely able to hide his relief.

Tom had obviously been in a coma for a very long time—months, possibly years. What could be seen of his face, half covered by a stained surgical mask, was old and grey, the skin stretched taut. His sunken eyes were closed, a build-up of crusty sleep clinging to the corners. His pepper-grey hair was matted and greasy, so long it snaked across the pillow in knotted clumps. His beard was longer still, a shaggy white mess that looked impervious to any comb.

His bony arms stretched out beside him, the translucent skin so thin the veins stood out like blue string. His slender fingers were tipped by long, untrimmed nails that curved gently back toward his palms. Yet despite his messy appearance, he had about him an extraordinary otherworldliness, as if they'd stumbled across some living relic from another time. Alex had an unsettling feeling that he'd somehow, somewhere met the man before. It was as if, little by little, he was reconnecting with his past, albeit a past he still knew very little about.

"It smells like death in here!" proclaimed Sarah as she opened the room's only window.

The surgical mask covering Tom's face was on the receiving end of a tube connected to a large brown bottle hanging from a shelf above the bed. A tiny droplet of fluid dribbled onto it every few seconds, giving it its stained appearance.

Sarah dabbed the end of the tube with a finger and lifted it to her nose. "Ewph!" she said, screwing up her face in disgust. "Ether! It's an anesthetic. Here, take a whiff."

Before Alex could protest, Sarah thrust her hand under his nose. The sweet, acrid odour—similar to the fluid Red McPhee used for his cigar lighter—stung his nostrils.

Alex wasted no time tugging the mask off Tom's face before flinging it into a corner of the room in disgust. He turned off the small tap administering the ether and ripped the tube off the wall. Almost immediately he noticed a slight change in Tom's breathing.

Sarah lifted one of Tom's hands, inspecting the long, gnarly fingernails. "He's going to pull through, I just know it. When he does, we don't want him to know how bad he looked. Keep an eye on him, I'll be right back," she said, leaving Alex to watch over Tom as he wondered what Sarah was up to.

She returned soon after with a bucket of warm soapy water, a sponge, towel, scissors, and a comb. Lifting up Tom's arms, she instructed Alex to pull back the bed sheets. Ripping them off briskly, Sarah gasped in shock, then giggled. In addition to his extremely crumpled pyjamas, Tom sported the kind of woolly socks normally worn by workmen—grey, with patches of white on the heel and toes. His toenails, however, had grown so long they'd sliced through the end.

"They're like curly claws!" said Sarah.

Alex watched curiously as Sarah went to work and attempted to cut through a thick, three-inch-long toenail first using one hand, then two, as her face reddened from the effort. With a loud snick, the toenail finally snapped. A large piece of it flashed across the room, hitting Alex on the cheek with such force it nicked his skin.

"Ouch!" he said, clutching his face. "Hey, I'm out of here before I lose an eye!"

As he made for the door, Alex's foot stubbed against something weighty sticking out from under the bed. Dropping to his knees, he discovered a case of dynamite. "Wow! Windlemore really didn't like him much." Stooping to pick up the heavy box, he staggered out the door with it, all the while trying his best not to shake its contents.

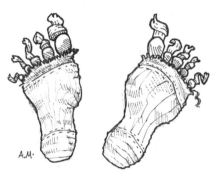

"Be careful," said Sarah. "We're too young to die."

Sweating nervously as he carried the dynamite delicately down the stairway, Alex placed the dangerous load gently by the doorway in the main hallway, half expecting it to blow up at any moment. By the time he'd finished scouring the treehouse for more explosives, he'd collected enough dynamite, gunpowder, and rifles to destroy Wid Dewr many times over.

Before returning to Sarah and Tom, Alex decided to revisit the radio room, which he'd discovered at the top of the treehouse while searching for explosives. Eager for a second look, he made his way quickly up the narrow staircase to the sturdy shed-like structure built around the very top of the tree.

Pulling up a seat beside the large radio—it was old even for 1929—Alex used the instrument's fist-sized dial to scan the airwaves for news from the outside world. Finding mostly static, he quickly realized Wildeor was out of range to all but the most powerful of transmitters. After a few minutes searching, he finally located a faint signal from

WQEW, a radio station out of New York. Alex sat back and listened keenly to the high-pitched tones of the presenter, his voice crackling through the static. Along with sports news and a brief item regarding sightings of unidentified animals in the border regions between Canada and the United States—he was no longer surprised at such reports—Alex found the following news item of interest:

DR. HUGH ECKENER OF GERMANY TODAY ANNOUNCED THAT AFTER THE *GRAF ZEPPELIN*'S SUCCESSFUL TRANS-ATLANTIC FLIGHT, THE AIRSHIP IS READY TO ATTEMPT THE FIRST CIRCUMNAVIGATION OF THE GLOBE. THE ANNOUNCEMENT CAME JUST A DAY AFTER THE GIANT OF THE AIR COMPLETED ITS THREE-DAY VOYAGE FROM EUROPE TO LAKEHURST NAVAL AIR STATION IN NEW JERSEY. THE AIRSHIP WILL SPEND THE NEXT FEW DAYS ON TRIALS PRIOR TO DEPARTING FROM NEW YORK.

Alex wished more than anything he could have been a part of the incredible event just announced. But he knew this was impossible. Nevertheless, he was thrilled to have heard the exciting news. Setting the receiver back to its original wavelength, he was surprised to hear a faint voice crackling through the static. Although speaking in an unfamiliar language, Alex did recognize Windlemore's name being used, leading him to conclude that someone was trying to signal the warden. Frustrated at his inability to understand the message, Alex turned the radio off and continued his exploration of the uppermost section of the treehouse.

Climbing a steep, winding staircase, he found himself in a brightly lit room, at the centre of which was a large, three-dimensional relief map of Wildeor. The level of detail was unlike anything Alex had ever imagined possible in so small a scale. He could make out the tiniest of features, from the buildings along the water's edge, the wooden submarine, the trees—even miniatures of the animals he encountered. Curiously, a series of small flags attached to pins had been placed at various locations on the map. Upon closer inspection, each depicted a species of the animal he'd seen marked Mortuus in The Beast of Wildeor. To his horror, two flags had been placed in the middle of Lake Idlerow, each with an image of a sea dragon on it. Windlemore, he realized, was using the map to plan his program of extermination, and Alex was horrified by the revelation that the sea dragons were earmarked for destruction.

Still shaken by this new evidence, Alex headed up to the observation level, the highest point of the treehouse. Climbing the tight, spiral staircase, he pushed open the hatch leading to the viewing platform. In the middle of the observation deck was a raised platform, on top of which stood a podium-like structure supporting a rather old—and rather odd—telescope. Looking like an oversized pair of binoculars, the device was at least four feet long and was affixed to the podium by a sturdy shaft.

Swivelling the device in a 360-degree arc, he was rewarded with a much-magnified panoramic view of Wildeor. Scanning Lake Idlerow, he looked for a sign of his sea dragon, but without success. He then watched with pleasure as Windlemore closed the hatch of the *Argonaut* and steamed away from the docks. Submerging slowly so only the conning tower was visible, the small submarine headed directly toward a large opened gate located in the rock face behind Wid Dewr.

"Good riddance to bad rubbish!" he muttered as the vessel disappeared from view. Taking a last look through the telescope, Alex enjoyed the unending sea of trees framed by the huge cloud-shrouded mountains. In the midst of it all, the two lakes—Idlerow and the much smaller moat around Wid Dewr—sparkled in the sunlight. It was the most spectacular of backdrops, and was no doubt one of the reasons he felt such a deep sense of belonging in Wildeor. He longed to spend a lifetime exploring every corner of it, but so much depended upon the events of the next few days.

It was with such thoughts rattling around his head that Alex rejoined Sarah to share the news of Windlemore's departure. What he saw as he entered Tom's bedroom was nothing short of miraculous. The old man's hair was now short and tidy, as was his neatly trimmed beard.

Sarah stood back to admire her handiwork. "I even gave him a manicure," she boasted proudly, holding up a hand for Alex's inspection. "And he's not so cold and clammy. Just look at the colour in his cheeks!"

Turning to Alex with a look of triumph, she added: "I think he's going to make it."

CHAPTER 14

LOST AND FOUND

"What do you mean, gone? He's in no condition to go any-where!" said Alex in disbelief. "That's impossible!" he added as he dashed up the stairs to see for himself.

Sure enough, Tom's bed was empty. He was about to question Sarah further when he heard the unmistakable sound of a toilet flushing. His jaw nearly hit the floor when the old man emerged seconds later through a small doorway neither he nor Sarah had previously noticed. Still in his crumpled pyjamas, he was also wearing a faded purple smoking jacket and a pair of well-worn moccasins. Alex considered the physical transformation nothing short of a miracle: although slightly stooped and frail, his eyes sparkled with life and energy.

"What?" he asked innocently. "It's been a long, long time!"

"You're . . . you're OK?" asked Alex, mystified by the radical change that had occurred.

"Was that a question or a statement?" asked Tom, his voice earthy and ageless with just a hint of an English accent. "Of course I'm OK! Why wouldn't I be?"

Tom patted his stomach. "Feeling a bit peckish, though. Be a dear girl and find me something to nibble on, would you? Oh, and a new pair of socks would be nice, too . . . these," he added, lifting a foot out of a moccasin, "have holes in them. And you, young man, can get me some water. Lots of water!"

"Uh, sure," said Alex, still a little perplexed. "But, um, shouldn't we introduce ourselves? I'm—"

"No need. I know exactly who you are. And, therefore, you know who I—" A loud gurgling in Tom's stomach caused him to stop mid-sentence. "Oh my," he said, turning back toward the concealed washroom. "Meet me in the library. So much to talk about." he said, slamming the door behind him.

Although puzzled by the old man's rapid recovery, Alex was thrilled to see him up as he set about his assigned task. Tom even beat them to the library: when they arrived, he was already making himself comfortable in the room's only chair, a large, wingback affair with elaborately carved arms and legs.

"Why is it every time you see me you look so surprised, Mr. Mortimer?" asked Tom.

Alex shrugged his shoulders, unsure quite what to say. "It's . . . well, you seem to have recovered so quickly."

"I've dealt with far worse than Windlemore over the years."

"But you were in pretty bad shape when we found you," said Sarah. "I tidied you up as best I could."

"For that I thank you," said Tom gratefully. "Not only do I look good, I feel good. Like a king who's just been given his kingdom back."

"That chair certainly looks like a throne," said Alex.

Tom smiled. Motioning them to place the food and drink on the table beside him, he stood and lifted the chair's cushioned seat, revealing a sturdy, round porcelain potty. "Not quite the kind of throne you were thinking of, I'm sure. Pretty useful before we put in the plumbing. Ha ha . . . nothing like a little toilet humour to lighten the mood." he said chuckling as he again made himself comfortable.

Alex laughed at the old man's wit, relieved that he was so very different to Windlemore.

Tom spent the next few minutes scrutinizing Alex and Sarah in turn, harrumphing and hmming to himself. Alex felt a wave of relief when the old man finally began quizzing them on everything that had happened since they'd met Mop at Mortimer's Point. After listening intently to their story, absorbing all they'd said, he again fell silent.

When he did eventually speak, it was in a gentle, hushed tone. "I take full responsibility for everything you've been through, as well as the terrible predicament we now find ourselves in. I was foolish not to pay closer attention to what's been going on. Now, I fear, it may all be too late."

"Too late for what?" asked Alex.

Tom looked at Alex glumly. "Too late to stop them."

Sarah crossed her arms, clearly unhappy with Tom's pessimistic tone. "You dragged us halfway across the continent for nothing? Mop promised you'd help find my parents, and keep us safe. Or did he just say that to shut us up?"

Tom smiled. "Your parents told me you were feisty! 'Never afraid of a fight,' they said. Excellent! We need some spirit."

"So you will help me find them?" she insisted.

Tom sighed deeply. "I'll try, Sarah. But only time will tell if we shall succeed. And time, I fear, is running out."

Tom then turned his attention to Alex. "What about you, Alex? Is there any fight left in you? You've been through so much, all those years spent with that dreadful Puddle woman."

"It's Pudsley," corrected Alex.

"Of course it is! I remember her all too well. It was I who arranged everything after your mother . . . well, after that terrible tragedy. I had no idea Mrs. Whatnot would prove so untrustworthy."

Alex sat bolt upright at the mention of his mother. "You knew her?"

Tom held his hand out to Alex. To his surprise, the old man dropped a rather plain gold ring into his palm. "It was your mother's. I've been keeping it safe until you were old enough to come and get it. And, well, here you are."

Alex took the ring, thrilled at having been given something that once belonged to his mother. Eagerly, he tried to squeeze it onto his middle finger, but was disappointed to get it only as far as the first knuckle. But the moment he gave up trying to force it on, the ring somehow expanded enough to slide all the way on. It was as if it had a will of its own, which Alex, of course, knew was impossible. But when he tried to pull it off, it wouldn't budge.

Alex's eyes welled up with tears at the thought of the mother he never knew. The ring somehow seemed to bring her closer.

"Keep it safe, Alex," said Tom with a knowing smile. "You may find it useful one of these days."

"What . . .what was she like?"

"A kinder, more compassionate person never walked this earth. Her loss was a terrible blow—" Tom's voice trailed off as if recalling some distant memory.

When he did eventually speak again, it was in a serious tone like that of a schoolteacher. "I'm afraid I must give you a rather lengthy history lesson," he said. "It's necessary in order that you fully understand the significance of the events of these past few days. This knowledge will prove crucial to your future survival. In fact, to the survival of all of us. Are you up to it?"

Alex nodded enthusiastically. Sarah did, too, although she managed to sneak in one further question.

"I hope you don't mind me asking. But how old are you?"

With what Alex would soon learn was his trademark humour, Tom simply said: "Perhaps you'd like to cut off my leg and count the rings?"

CHAPTER 15

A RATHER LONG HISTORY LESSON

The weather was already changing as Tom settled down to share the story of Wildeor. The last traces of daylight were obscured by an impenetrable black cloud, and the breeze from the lake had developed into a strong wind—so strong that even the huge golden oak, Wid Dewr, creaked and groaned like an old ship.

Tom's recovery had affected Alex profoundly, filling him with new hope. It seemed each passing minute only energized the old man further. He was, Alex could tell, quite extraordinary in every sense of the word.

"So, where shall we start?" asked Tom.

Alex shot his hand up like an eager schoolboy. "At the beginning! The very beginning."

"Very well. The beginning it is."

And so it was, as Tom began his extraordinary tale, that Alex finally learned the truth behind his hitherto unhappy life.

"The earth," said Tom, "was once a paradise, crafted by the Great Power for his favourite creations."

"What great pow—ow!" Alex winced as Sarah whacked him.

"Butt in again and I'll really give you something to cry about," she said. "Let the man finish."

Tom did his best to ignore the interruption. "Only the Keepers, ordained to care for Earth's many wonderful life forms, ever saw the Great Power. That was how it began, and how it should have remained."

"Were these Keepers human?" asked Alex, but not before shuffling out of Sarah's reach.

Tom smiled kindly. "They were like humans in some ways, such as their appearance. But they were perhaps a little more like the beings you call angels."

"Were they immortal like angels?" asked Sarah.

"Not exactly. But we'll get to that later."

"Many magnificent temples," he continued, "were built in homage to the Great Power. Places like Aslintas, Thersden, Vahalla. Some still exist, many more have been destroyed or forgotten. The Keepers kept some of the most magnificent of beasts at these sacred places: fiery land dragons, and sleek sea dragons that swam the oceans in great schools. Rarest of all was the colossal winged dragon, the King of Beasts. These were magnificent heavenly creatures, formed from the very essence of the Great Power himself.

"As the human population grew, new Keepers were fashioned from the stars to watch over them. But there was one who didn't turn out like the others: it was as if he was cast from a different mould, lacking empathy and reason. Above all else, he felt little love for mankind.

"Despite the protests of the other Keepers, the Great Power came to favour this unusual being. Eventually, he was named the Highest Keeper and given the task of watching over Earth while the Great Power's attention was focused elsewhere."

Alex again raised his hand to get Tom's attention, adding a loud cough after the old man initially failed to acknowledge him.

With an exasperated sigh, Tom finally asked: "What now, Alex?"

"But there's only one Earth. Where else could he focus his attention?"

"There are more stars and planets than there are grains of sand on all the beaches of the world. Have you therefore never considered there may be others like you out there?"

"God help us, no!" said Sarah. "One of him is more than enough."

It was now Alex's turn to swat Sarah.

Tom rose unsteadily from his chair. "You two are quite the pair. I could do with a break."

"But we've only just started," complained Sarah.

"All that water, I'm afraid—"

With Tom out of earshot, Sarah turned to Alex and said: "Gosh! Sir Talks-a-lot or what? It's a bit far-fetched, don't you think? Maybe all that ether's gone to his head."

"What about the Wendigo? He didn't make that up. And Boggy?" Alex nudged the Sasquatch as it lay curled in a ball, sound asleep, by his feet.

"Don't be silly. Boggy's just a strange little monkey. Things like him are discovered all the time. It all sounds like something out of Sunday School, though with a unique new twist."

"Well, I believe Tom even if you don't," said Alex.

"It's not that I don't believe him. It's just . . . well, he's so old and . . . and decrepit. I think he might even have dementia."

"Dementia, eh?" interrupted Tom as he walked back into the room. "Maybe so, young lady. But my hearing's still pretty sharp. Just because you can't see something doesn't mean it's not there. It takes faith to believe in the unbelievable."

Tom settled back in his chair. "Where were we?"

"Sorry, Tom," said Sarah sheepishly. "You just introduced the new Keeper."

"Ah, yes. Glad someone was paying attention. No more interruptions! There's much to get through before that conniving Windlemore gets back.

"Over time, the Great Power lost interest in this world. As his influence declined, mankind began to worship other things, such as wealth, power, and possessions.

"A change came over the Highest Keeper, too. He came to understand that for all things there was an opposite—for light, there was darkness, for love there was hate. What he learned resonated, and he began dabbling in ever-darker things, all the while believing he could control the dark. He was wrong. Slowly, surely, the darkness took control, fuelling the resentment and hatred that burned within, poisoning his soul with an impenetrable blackness. His heart grew cold, and he came to believe the world should revere him as it had once revered the Great Power.

"It was then that he adopted the name by which he would forever be known: Ultimus. His first act of treachery was to corrupt the White Dragon, the most magnificent of the winged dragons. His name was Athoran, the King of Beasts. Slowly, Ultimus poisoned Athoran with his dark thoughts, eventually turning beast against beast, and, worse still, beast against man.

"Ultimus next turned his attention to the Keepers themselves. Some he corrupted with the same black magic that had corrupted him, encouraging them in turn to pervert the beasts in their care. All the while, he secretly prepared to unleash his wrath upon the world.

"Confident his time had come, he summoned the Keepers to the oldest and most important of the places of worship, the Temple of the Hanging Stones. You will know it as Stonehenge. He lured them with a promise that the Great Power, after an absence of many centuries, would return, and instructed them to bring their most prized beasts. Even those still wary of Ultimus and his motivations were unable to resist the desire to see their maker. It was an incredible sight as thousands of the most splendid creatures gathered together. And with them came the Keepers and their entourages, as well as the greatest Chieftains amongst the many tribes of men, all waiting expectantly."

Tom paused. Alex sensed the heaviness weighing upon the old man as he told his story. After a few moments of silence, he nudged Tom's leg gently. "You OK?"

"Hmm? What? Oh yes . . . yes . . . sorry."

"You were describing the scene at Stonehenge."

"Stonehenge? Yes, of course. Thank you Alex.

"Making a dramatic entrance upon Athoran, Ultimus addressed the excited gathering, announcing that the time had come for the Great Power to reveal himself. Then, commanding Athoran to bow down before him, he declared that he himself was the new Great Power, and that all who stood in his way would be destroyed. Placing his hands upon Athoran, the crowds watched in disbelief and horror as the magnificent hide turned from pure white to jet black.

"A horde of heavily armed warriors then swarmed forward, viciously attacking the defenceless gathering. These were the Ultima, a group of heartless men raised to do the bidding of their dark lord, led by the most corrupt of the Keepers. It was soon evident that no evil was beyond them, no deed too vile, as they wielded their newfound power.

"As the crowds fled, Athoran took to the air, joined by other Black Dragons brought under Ultimus's spell. With incredible savagery, they swooped, spewing a deadly black poison from their mouths, choking the life out of all living things. Massive armour-clad land dragons spread out in all directions, incinerating anything that stood in their path.

"The great Red Dragon, Iddraig, rose up against Athoran. It was a terrible sight to behold as the two beasts fought ferociously, one in an attempt to stop further slaughter, the other to commit it. The battle between Athoran and Iddraig moved quickly across the countryside as they fought, finally coming to a terrible climax at a place called Dinas Emrys."

Tom paused once more, the same sorrow pressing upon him that Alex noticed earlier. It was as if the old man were reliving the things about which he spoke, perhaps recalling some personal loss. But this, Alex believed, was impossible, and he soon dismissed the thought as Tom continued.

"The Red Dragon was no more, and with his demise the hopes of mankind were dashed. Tens of thousands perished during that day of bloodshed, and many more lost their lives as the terror spread. Those that resisted were destroyed or enslaved. Some, anxious to survive, joined Ultimus as the earth was plunged into a cold, inhospitable dark age.

"Although a handful of Keepers managed to evade extermination, countless beasts were hunted to extinction. Magnificent creatures like the great dragons of the Middle Kingdoms, the winged horses of Olympus, such splendid creatures, all destroyed. Few beasts, apart from the abominations dreamt up by Ultimus, survived his terror. Those that did were forced to hide in the most remote corners of the world, rarely to be seen again. Ultimus, it seemed, wanted to erase every sign of the Great Power.

"The few surviving Keepers who had not succumbed to Ultimus attempted to rally mankind to fight back, but their efforts amounted to nothing. The remaining Chieftains had become wary of them, blaming them for the terrible evil that had descended upon the earth. In desperation, these Keepers searched for a leader capable of uniting all mankind. But treachery, it seemed, existed even within this small group, and each attempt to find a suitable leader was thwarted.

"Few Chieftains survived the Betrayal, as the slaughter at Stonehenge became known. Those who did were hunted like animals or were forced into slavery by Ultimus. But it was from the descendants of those who had fled that the remaining Keepers hoped to find a leader. They searched in vain for many years, until one of them, Myrddin, encountered an all-but-forgotten village at the edge of the known world. After Myrddin shared his story with the villagers, an elder told him of a Chieftain from afar who had sought refuge with them many years earlier. Travelling with him was a woman and a child, a boy. They did not stay long for fear of capture, and so purchased a small fishing vessel to continue their journey westward. The vessel was later discovered abandoned near an island that was reputedly home to an old witch and that was considered cursed.

"Upon hearing this tale, Myrddin made his way to the desolate island the old man spoke of, eventually finding it shrouded in an impenetrable mist. Climbing the crumbling stairs to a large cave in the sea cliff, he found the withered remains of the old witch, long since dead. Resting on a bed close by, and covered by a thick shroud, was the body of a child. Removing the shroud, Myrddin revealed a seemingly lifeless boy of about five years of age. In his hand was clasped a small vial of liquid. Believing it contained an antidote to whatever had caused the boy's decades-long slumber, Myrddin poured the contents into the boy's mouth. Moments later, the boy awoke, frightened and with no recollection of who he was or how he'd come to be there.

"Far from the Ultima, Myrddin raised Artur, as the boy had been named, as best he could. Over time, the boy grew to love and respect the Keeper as he would have his own father. But being a Keeper, fatherhood was foreign to him, and he had to quickly learn how to raise first a child, then a teenager, and finally a young man. But he persevered, recognizing that destiny had brought them together for a reason: Artur would be the one to unite mankind against Ultimus. He was tenacious, curious, quick-witted and intelligent, and possessed a keen sense of justice along with an intense distaste for evil.

"Myrddin trained the boy in the ways of the Keepers as well as those of man. But Artur matured to manhood slowly, over a period of decades rather than years. This at first confused the Keeper, until he discovered, through writings left behind by the old witch, that the water from a nearby spring possessed unique mineral qualities that dramatically slowed the aging process. This suited Myrddin well, allowing time for the boy to develop and train until ready to fulfil his destiny.

"Myrddin had prepared well for what would be a bitter struggle. To ensure at least a small chance of victory, he and Artur made secret sorties to Stonehenge and other once important sites to scavenge for items needed in their fight against Ultimus, and to prepare the way for Artur's arrival. They also began a campaign of guerrilla warfare, hitting the Ultima hard and unexpectedly where they were weak, always leaving a trademark calling card—the initials AR, usually carved into the chest or forehead of a dead Ultima warrior."

"Ew, that's horrible!" said Sarah, now as entranced by Tom's story as Alex. "But why AR?"

"It stood for Artur Rex," replied Tom. "It means—"

"King Arthur!" exclaimed Sarah, excitedly. "So he wasn't just a legend?"

"He was as real as you or I," said Tom. "Or at least, Artur was."

"Why would Myrddin want the Ultima to think Artur . . . King Arthur . . . was doing this?" asked Alex.

"To let Ultimus know there was someone capable of challenging him. It would cost him many restless nights, as it did the Ultima and the Black Dragons. A sleep-deprived enemy is one that makes mistakes. As you're about to learn, Myrddin knew Ultimus's weaknesses, and how to exploit them.

"Myrddin hoped above all else to find Caldwulf, a sword that had belonged to Nathon, the first of the Keepers, but lost after his death during the Betrayal. Forged by the Great Power, the sword's original purpose was symbolic. But Caldwulf had fallen into the hands of Ultimus, who now kept it hidden, using it only to sacrifice those who stood against him. For it was known that only the Great Power—or items forged by him, like Caldwulf—could end the life of a Keeper.

Myrddin also visited Dinas Emrys, where he undertook the gruesome task of recovering portions of the hide from Iddraig, the Red Dragon. Most of the remains had long since rotted away, but in a deep pool he found a small section of the beast's flesh, preserved by the icy cold water. He later forged the iridescent scales from the dragon's skin into powerful amulets, each imbued with a trace of the once great creature's power."

"What, these things?" Alex asked excitedly, pulling his amulet from his shirt.

Tom leant forward, grasping the jewel in his hands, inspecting it carefully. "Precisely those amulets. You've no doubt noticed how they change colour? The Red Dragon's powers were those of the elements, which is why you'll see it change from fire red to deepest blue, and all shades in between. Myrddin was only able to fashion eleven, and consequently they are highly sought after by people like Windlemore, who I regret to say was given one. They are a powerful defence against any animal that might want to cause harm."

"But not a Wendigo, apparently?" said Sarah cynically.

"The Wendigo isn't an animal. It's a twisted, evil spirit that wears the flesh of its victims."

"So that's why it smelt so bad," said Alex.

"Exactly. It takes a very different power to deal with such evil, the same evil as is found in Ultimus."

Tom seemed to consider his next words carefully. "There's still so much to tell, and time is running out. Windlemore's up to something, I can sense it. What time is it, Alex?"

Alex retrieved his watch from the breast pocket of his shirt. "It's eight thirty on the dot."

"Good! We'll soon have this wrapped up."

"Tom, I've been thinking," said Alex. "If Artur really was King Arthur, does that mean Myrddin was—"

"Merlin?" said Tom, finishing the question. "Smart chap! I wondered which of you would figure that out, though to be honest my money was on Sarah. Full of surprises, aren't you, Alex?"

"Um, thanks . . . I think."

"Neither Arthur or Merlin—Artur or Myrddin—were anything like the characters you'll have heard of. It was all part of a program of misinformation aimed at concealing the truth about what really happened. And, to some extent, what's still happening today. But more about that later. Let's get this history lesson out of the way so we can talk about the present . . . and, perhaps more importantly, the future. Your future! Now, where was I? Ah, yes—"

CHAPTER 16

THE LORDS OF ALLEGIANCE

"The Lords of what?" asked Alex.

"The Lords of Allegiance," said Tom.

Then it clicked. Alex had seen a reference to the Lords of Allegiance while researching the sea dragons in *The Beasts of Wildeor*. "Tell me more!" he said eagerly.

Tom nodded, and continued with his history lesson.

"After locating the last of the Keepers—no more than a handful had survived Ultimus's purge—Artur and Myrddin sought the strongest, bravest and wisest of the remaining Chieftains. Together they forged the Lords of Allegiance, an alliance whose purpose was to defeat the Ultima. The Allegiance set about secretly recruiting a small army, but Myrddin knew they couldn't yet defeat the Ultima on the battlefield. Their only chance was to deprive Ultimus of his source of power, the Orbs of Orion. Forged from elements of the heavens by the Great Power, these celestial lights—so powerful they could turn a man to dust if he so much as glanced at them—were seized by Ultimus after the Betrayal. They were kept at Stonehenge, each one placed atop the eleven large stone pillars erected in the middle of the massive temple. Separately, they were nothing more than curiosities, but together they gave Ultimus the power to rule the earth.

"In the middle of the stone circle was the altar upon which Ultimus sacrificed his enemies. This, too, was a source of his grip over humanity and the dark beasts held under his sway. Myrddin knew that if he could break the circle of light and destroy the altar, Ultimus's reign of terror could be ended.

"The plan to defeat Ultimus was a perilous one, but it was the only chance they had to rid the world of evil. While the main forces of the Lords of Allegiance led their troops in a diversionary attack on the key Ultima stronghold of Aslintas, Myrddin and Artur would strike at the heart of Ultimus's power. Myrddin had a unique gift bestowed upon him by the Great Power. He was a Soul Shifter, able to occupy inanimate objects or the bodies of the dead. He guarded this secret from all but Artur. Myrddin also kept another secret: he took over the body of a dead Chieftain loyal to Ultimus who had been killed in a skirmish with the Allegiance.

"He knew Ultimus was unaware of the Chieftain's death. If Ultimus saw Myrddin in the body of the Chieftain, Ultimus would grant him an audience, especially as he intended to have the infamous AR—Artur Rex—with him as a prisoner. With Artur feigning capture, Myrddin would lead him to Ultimus, who was eager to torment the man who would be king. The plan worked. As Myrddin hoped, Ultimus ignored him as he focused his attention on Artur.

"Unobserved, Myrddin searched for Caldwulf, the sword that would prove their only hope. It was then that Artur cast off his chains and challenged Ultimus. Although caught by surprise, Ultimus quickly gained the upper hand. The clash took a terrible toll upon Artur and he soon collapsed, apparently beaten, to the ground. While Ultimus gloated, Myrddin found Caldwulf. Placing the sword within Artur's reach, Myrddin then swiftly broke the circle of orbs, leaving Ultimus vulnerable. Artur plunged the sword into Ultimus's chest. Injured, Ultimus collapsed, leaving Artur the opportunity to strike the final blow. But something stopped him. The anger, the fury, the hatred were all emotions he recognized as the kind Ultimus possessed, and he wanted no part of it. Instead, binding the weakened Ultimus tightly in ropes and chains, he presented him to Myrddin.

"Although Myrddin wanted Ultimus dead, he couldn't bring himself to do it either. The same capacity for compassion and pity the Great Power had bestowed upon mankind was also within him. Recognizing this, Myrddin used his powers as a Soul Shifter to cast Ultimus's spirit from his body, which he then destroyed. Ultimus's black, hateful soul was sealed for all time in a crypt hidden far from prying eyes, shrouded in secrecy. Only he and Artur knew where."

Tom paused to replenish his glass.

Alex was spellbound by the exciting tale. Before Tom could again speak, he asked a question that seemed to catch the old man by surprise.

"Where did they send Ultimus?"

Tom seemed to ponder the question carefully. "Aslintas," he finally answered. "Perhaps better known today—and incorrectly, I might add—as Atlantis.

"Hang on," said Sarah. "You said only Myrddin and Artur knew where he was imprisoned?"

Tom simply stared at his moccasins, saying nothing.

Sarah looked at him quizzically. "Wait a minute . . . You're King Arthur?"

"No he's not!" blurted Alex excitedly. "He's Myrddin. Or Merlin. That's why you know so much about all this stuff, isn't it? Because you were there!"

Tom smiled awkwardly. "Yes, I am indeed Myrddin. But Merlin? Well, not so much."

"What do you mean? Aren't Myrddin and Merlin one and the same?" asked Sarah.

"Not exactly. How much do you know about the Arthurian legend?"

"Only that no one seems to know for sure whether they really existed."

"Until now!" added Alex.

"My point exactly. No one knows for sure because there's no proof. Why is there no proof? I'll tell you why . . . because it's been hidden, or destroyed."

Alex was confused. "What do you mean?"

"It took centuries to erase the evidence of those years of terror under Ultimus, and Artur's triumph over him."

"Why on earth would you want to do that?" asked Sarah.

"Because mankind finds it so very difficult to resist the darkness. And, of course, there were the beasts to think of. They needed—and still need—protecting."

Tom paused, as if relishing some age-old memory. "People just lapped it up. It was so easy back then to spin a tale. A few words whispered in the ear of an elder or storyteller, and whomph, the story would spread like wildfire, keeping people's attention away from what was really going on."

"What was really going on?" asked Alex, his curiosity aroused.

"Let me wrap up this tale and everything will make sense, I promise. With Ultimus gone, the Ultima eventually collapsed as the Lords of Allegiance led mankind to victory. Artur was triumphant, the world finally free of darkness. It was as if the Great Power had returned! Artur led the hunt for the remaining Ultima and their beasts including the dragon Athoran. It was in fact the blood of that fearsome beast that almost killed him, a poison that would cause him great discomfort in future years.

"After the first War of Allegiance, those of our beasts that were not destroyed in the fighting, or by Ultimus, were sent to isolated corners of the world where they could be hidden away and kept from doing harm, and kept from harm.

"As time passed, so, too, did the influence of the Allegiance. The world was changing, its population growing so rapidly it became increasingly difficult to protect the remaining beasts. Men were no longer fearful of the wild places where beasts were safe. They were also no longer interested in untamed creatures, favouring domesticated animals that were easier to raise and far more predictable.

"The Lords of Allegiance therefore set themselves one last task: to deal with the surviving beasts. And so I . . . I mean, Myrddin . . . extended his program of misinformation to muddy the truth even further regarding these amazing and once-common creatures. Our plan was straightforward enough: set up safe havens where the remaining Keepers could retreat with the beasts, far from mankind's prying eyes until such time as they could be reintroduced.

"A ledger of all beasts was made. This is *The Book of Beasts*. In addition, two further ledgers were kept. The *Book of Allegiance* was a record of the history of the Lords of Allegiance, and tracked each member's history along with their lineage throughout the years. The third—the name of which escapes me for the moment—was created as a record of everything of importance to the Lords of Allegiance—the sword Caldwulf, the Orbs of Orion, the altar from Stonehenge, Aslintas—where they were, what they were useful for, that sort of thing."

"I've seen *The Beasts of Wildeor*," said Alex excitedly. "Is that anything like *The Book of Beasts*?"

"Yes, but it's local to Wildeor. *The Book of Beasts* is every creature that is and ever was. It contains details of where to find those species that still exist, and the last known whereabouts of those now extinct. Which, sadly, is most of them. I have The *Book of Allegiance*, but the whereabouts of the other two remain a mystery. So many years have passed, and with the constant moving, things get lost, I'm afraid."

"What do you mean, moving?" asked Sarah. "Haven't you always been here in Wildeor?"

"Dear me, no. I only moved here about, oh, let me see—" Tom started counting on his fingers, but soon gave up. "Oh, about two thousand years ago. Not long, really."

"And before that?" asked Alex.

"Cymru, or Wales as it is perhaps better known. Beautiful place called Hafod. Then Ireland, followed by a spell in Scandinavia—those magnificent fjords! That was followed by various locations across the Americas before finally settling here—which I sincerely hope will be my final stop. There are so few places to hide these days. And moving is so very tiring. At my age, I deserve a rest. Which is exactly what I was doing before all this Ultima nonsense flared up again."

Sarah sighed loudly. "Tom, no disrespect, but are you serious? I mean, did all this stuff really happen? Even if it did, what's it got to do with us?"

Tom got up and made his way to the bookcase. Pulling out one of the larger books, he uncovered a secret handle that enabled the bookcase to be opened like a door. Behind it was a large walk-in closet. Alex at first mistook the garments it contained as costumes from a theatre company: there were old Roman togas and uniforms; fancy military jackets; hats, helmets and headdresses; even a collection of wigs.

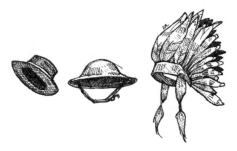

"Windlemore would never go near this closet. Look at all this lovely dust! He hates dust with a passion," said Tom, rifling through the clothing like a bargain hunter in a dime store. "Aha! Here it is." He pulled out a heavy, grey woollen coat that wouldn't have looked out of place on a Highland shepherd. "Dustiest, mustiest thing I could find! And here," he said, reaching into the coat's lining, "is the very thing I'm looking for."

Tom placed an old Bible-thick book on the library's writing desk and beckoned Sarah and Alex to join him as he leafed through its aging, brown pages.

"This, my young friends, is The *Book of Allegiance*, something Windlemore would sorely like to get his dirty hands on. Now, let me see . . . E . . . F . . . here we are . . . G! Ga . . . Ge . . . " said Tom, sounding out each combination of letters. "Gi . . .G . . . ah ha! Gr for Greystone! There you go, see for yourself," he said, stabbing the page emphatically with his gnarly old index finger. "Told you so. Wrote the entry for your lot myself."

"What do you mean, your lot?" Sarah asked.

"We found your clan way up in the northernmost regions of what is today known as Scotland. They were hiding from the Ultima in the peat bogs. Scruffy bunch . . . which I see runs in the family," he added.

Ignoring Tom's comment, Sarah read the entry as instructed: "Greystone: Named for their ability to blend in with their surroundings using liberal coatings of bog mud and peat moss. Fearless warrior clan. Joined the Allegiance under the leadership of Adair Greystone, a natural leader whose fiery red hair was as long as his temper was short."

Alex sniggered. "Sounds like Sarah!"

Crossing her arms in a huff, Sarah sat down and listened to what Tom had to say about her ancestors.

"Adair was a remarkable man. Next to Artur, you couldn't ask for a better man on your side in a pickle. True of all Greystones, as far as I'm concerned. I'm sure you'll prove just as reliable."

Alex asked Tom about his heritage. "Ah, yes," said the old man, flipping speedily through the book. "The Mortimers were a rather more complex bunch than our simple friends the Greystones. Here we are—"

Tom stopped in the midst of the entries starting with the letter P. "But Mortimer starts with an M, not a P," said Alex.

Tom tapped the page indignantly to get Alex's attention. "Like I said, the Mortimers are complicated. Mortimer is in fact a relatively new name your ancestors adopted at my request some nine-hundred years or so ago. Largely for security reasons, you see. Read here . . . and here—"

"Pen Draig: Artur—" Alex stopped immediately, his heart racing as he looked at Tom quizzically. "Is this the Artur you spoke of? King Arthur?"

"Don't forget, he was never King Arthur. I did that to throw people off our scent. Worked a treat, as we already know. Now read on, there's a good chap."

"Later Pendragon. Birth date, unknown. Died 1666, aged approximately three-thousand five hundred and sixty-two years." Alex looked at Tom in disbelief. "How could he possibly have grown so old?"

"Old to you, perhaps," said Tom. "But to me he was but a child. Remember that water I mentioned? The spring that could keep a human young for a very, very long time?"

"I still don't get the connection," said Alex, perplexed.

"What he's trying to tell you is that your great-great-great-great-great-grandfather or something was King Arthur, or this Artur Pen Draig," said Sarah. "The same guy Tom—or Myrddin or Merlin or whatever you call yourself—fought with against Ultimus. Gosh, this is giving me a headache!"

"So . . . I'm related to Artur?" asked Alex.

Tom closed the book and took it with him back to his chair. "Yes, you are. You're his direct descendent, his living heir. This book needs some updating, but it proves a number of things: the existence of the Lords of Allegiance; that your parents are part of the Allegiance; and, ipso facto, by default, so are you . . . both of you. At least, you could be if you so choose."

"Gosh," said Alex.

"I need a bath!" said Sarah.

"And I," said Tom, "need the bathroom. Let's take a break and re-convene in an hour. I've taken far too much time as it is telling this story, no thanks to your interruptions, Mr. Mortimer. Gather your thoughts, and we'll next figure out how we're to deal with Windlemore when he returns—which will be soon, given how recklessly he operates that poor submarine."

"But there's more, isn't there?" asked Alex intuitively. "I mean, our parents? Will you tell us what happened to them. Please?"

Tom looked at Alex and Sarah with a troubled expression. "Very well, if I must. I believe you're ready. But first, let's take that break."

CHAPTER 17

ANSWERS TO PRETTY MUCH EVERYTHING

Settling down to hear the conclusion to Tom's story—his story—Alex was startled by the ferocity of the thunderstorm that now raged across Wildeor. Sarah sidled closer, never taking her eyes off the lightning flashing and flickering across the otherwise pitch-black sky.

"You're sure this tree's lightning proof?" she asked nervously.

Alex nodded, reminding her that he'd seen the sturdy lightning rod while inspecting the observation level of the treehouse. As keen as he was to question Tom further about his family, he suggested that Sarah ask about the fate of her parents first.

She began the moment the old man entered the room. "Are my parents going to be OK?"

Still dressed in his pyjamas and smoking jacket, Tom—always careful in his responses—took his time getting comfortable in the old armchair. "I can't say for sure. Thanks to Windlemore, I've been a little out of touch."

"What about Mop?" asked Alex. "You managed to get him to help."

"You mean Lonsdale? I was lucky there. He's well travelled and thinks a lot more creatively than most. His friendship with your parents certainly helped get him onside. The fog was his idea, too."

"Fog?" asked Sarah.

"The heavy mist shrouding the mountains around Wildeor," said Tom. "It was Lonsdale who suggested we tap into the hot springs in the mountains to create the fog that stops those new fangled flying machines from bothering us. Works a treat. Perhaps a little too well, as now even he can't fly through it. He did start building a machine to regulate the amount produced, but we need to get him back to finish it."

Tom paused, gathering his thoughts. "Anyway, back to the Greystones. Your parents were doing some research for me, Sarah. Africa is such a rich source of material for an archeologist. They were on the trail of three very important things: the missing orbs, and the missing books in the Wildeor trilogy."

"That's only two things," said Sarah.

"Yes, I know," said Tom. "The third is perhaps the greatest discovery ever made." Tom paused for effect. "Aslintas. Ultimus's final resting place."

"I thought you said you knew where Aslintas was?"

"Oh, I knew where it was," said Tom. "Trouble is, I don't know where it is. It was so very long ago, and the earth's crusty bits move around so much. Plates shift, mountains come and go, oceans rise and fall. The world looks very, very different today than it did all those millennia ago. The Ultima obviously don't know where it is, either, which is why they want that notebook. I'm positive that within its pages we'll find what we need to know regarding Aslintas. And we must get there before anyone else, whether Ultima or some rogue nation."

"You mean to say there are governments that know about Ultimus?" asked Sarah.

"Of course. Been a bit of a breakdown in communications in recent years, though. Many Lords of Allegiance have made themselves useful by gaining positions of power in order to influence governments and kingdoms. Sadly, so has the other side."

Tom adopted a more serious tone. "If the Ultima get hold of your parents' notebook and The *Book of Allegiance*, they'd know the whereabouts of the Orbs of Orion and other relics, too. They'll also know the names of everyone involved in the Allegiance. They'd hunt them down. We already have our hands full as we rebuild the Allegiance and safeguard the beasts and relics of the old order. And," he added, gesturing toward Alex and Sarah, "it won't be easy given the fact we are so few."

"We?" said Sarah, indignantly. "Why is it every time someone says we it involves Alex and I being chased?"

"Because you two are the trump cards," said Tom. "We'll just have to make sure they never get hold of you. Either of you."

"And how do you propose we do that?" asked Sarah.

"Time, patience . . . and a lot of luck."

"What role did my parents have in all this?" asked Alex.

"Well, as you already know, your father was a descendent of Artur, as are you. Therefore he and your mother became prime targets for a revived Ultima. Had we known better, we'd have taken greater measures to protect all of you. But there was no indication that the Ultima were on the rise. Your mother was in North America when the Great War broke out, a war of petty grievances no doubt fuelled by the Ultima. It was perhaps ill advised that she travel when the storm clouds were gathering, but such was her strength of character that no one, not even your father, could persuade her otherwise."

"Then why'd she do it?" asked Alex.

"A mother's desire to show off her children, and—" Tom's voice trailed off.

"And what"? asked Alex.

Tom sat up a little straighter in his chair. "There was the question of the beast. Every new heir to the Allegiance has a beast assigned to him, and their fates are in many ways entwined. Early on, we knew yours was special."

"How special?" asked Alex.

"Special enough that your mother would risk travelling during wartime. I should have stopped her from returning to England. She was adamant she should be with your father and so insisted her family—along with your beast—be shipped home, despite the risks. That ship was the *Lusitania*. Much of what actually happened is still a mystery, but the fact remains that your mother and sister were never found. You were placed in the care of a ship's officer, and arrangements made to keep you safe until such time as we could rebuild the Allegiance."

"What about my father?"

Tom paused. "Your father's disappearance still baffles me. After your mother's death, he became reckless. It was as if he had nothing more to live for. He was reported missing in No Man's Land a few months later. His body was never found. I'm sorry it's not a happier ending, Alex."

Although saddened by Tom's revelation, Alex was glad to have learned a little more about his parents. But the question of what happened to the beast—his beast—still bothered him. "What about the serpent? My beast?" he asked.

"You can't guess?"

Alex thought for a moment, then it clicked. "The serpent in Lake Idlerow!" he said, excitedly. "But how did it get back?"

"The continents and oceans are connected by networks of underwater passageways and tunnels. You call them fault lines. I've explored many since getting the *Argonaut*. The water beasts simply follow their homing instincts. Another reason why we keep them penned up. Yours returned a few weeks after the sinking, though looking worse for wear."

"You mean the scar?" asked Alex.

"Yes. It must have happened when the beast escaped the sinking ship."

"You keep calling him a beast? Does he have a name?"

"As the beast's Kindred Spirit, it's your job to choose a name for him," said Tom.

"Speaking of names," said Sarah. "How did you end up as Tom?"

Tom smiled. "Simple, really. I believe I mentioned the native people around these parts helped keep Wildeor a secret. As Wid Dewr grew into the spectacular tree it is now, I set up house in it. They thought me crazy. Most still do."

"Quelle surprise!" said Sarah. "Well, you are a little eccentric, aren't you?"

Tom chuckled as he took a pen and paper from his pocket. Scribbling down a few words, he passed the paper to Alex. It read: THE OLD MAN WHO LIVES IN A TREE.

"Tom. W. Liat!" said Alex, impressed.

"It does have a nice ring to it, doesn't it? A little more contemporary than Myrddin, too. People would mangle the name so terribly! Especially your Mrs. Pudding!"

"Speaking of Mrs. Pudsley," said Alex. "Why her?"

"He's right," said Sarah. "Hardly a good choice for a substitute parent. And whose idea was it to hide a Mortimer in a place called Mortimer's Point?"

"Guilty," said Tom. "That, too, was only meant to be temporary. We planned to have you brought to Wildeor, but I already doubted Windlemore's integrity. Then there was the issue of my declining health, which we now know was Windlemore's doing. Mrs. Piddlesly—"

"Pudsley!" corrected Alex.

"Quite, Mrs. Piddlepuddle, or whatever, never heard from us again and so just sort of carried on the best she could. Poor woman, wasn't all her fault. She really was desperately unhappy."

"Why didn't my parents intervene?" asked Sarah.

"They weren't involved at that stage. I was going to tell them about Alex when Windlemore interfered—"

Alex looked at Tom, a puzzled expression etched upon his face. "How could you have known Sarah and I were in Wildeor? You were in a coma—"

Sarah's face lit up. "Soul shifting! That's how you did it."

"Clever girl. Although my mind and body were incapacitated, my soul was free to wander, here and there finding opportunities to borrow, I guess you could say, the occasional body, or a suitable substitute. It took a while to convince your parents it was me."

"The stone giant! That was you, wasn't it?" said Alex.

Tom held up his hands in mock modesty. "Did the job, didn't it? Stopped those Ultima dead in their tracks. Pardon the pun. Put that Wendigo in its place, too."

It was now Sarah's turn to speak up. "Talking of that disgusting vile creature, what's with all those bones in the mountain?"

"And the weapons," said Alex.

"As evil as the Wendigo is, it does have its uses. Once Ultimus had been dealt with, Artur decided it was time to step aside. Taking the most important of the relics with us, along with the beasts in our care, we moved westward into the dense dark forests where men feared to venture. After Ultimus, you see, mankind had become tremendously fearful of the unknown: tales of evil creatures and strange monsters were widespread. It served us well, so we naturally encouraged this behaviour.

"Such was his fame, however, that we were never able to settle for long before some adventurer found where Artur was hiding. So we finally moved very, very far away, to this location. It became the stuff of legend."

Ever the scholar, Sarah piped up. "There was never any mention of King Arthur going to Wildeor. Only Avalon."

"Wildeor is the Avalon of legend," said Tom. "But we had to keep that hush-hush, because every now and then some small group of Ultima that had survived the War of Allegiance, or bandits or adventurers, would find us. From time to time they'd turn up—unannounced and unwelcome. Been going on for centuries. They still turn up from time to time."

"And the Wendigo?" asked Alex.

"Best guard dog you'd ever want. Insatiable appetite. The native peoples had been terrorized by it for centuries, so when I promised to take care of it for them, they were more than happy to turn a blind eye to what we were doing in Wildeor. A strategically placed Wendigo certainly took care of any interlopers."

"And Artur?" asked Sarah

"He did eventually pass on, but not before living a very, very long time. He took such delight in the tales spun about him. Made many of them up himself—Lancelot and the Lady of the Lake were his favourites. He even joined me from time to time on expeditions back to places like Stonehenge, often clandestinely visiting the family he left behind."

Sarah perked up at the mention of family. "He was married?"

"Yes, but outliving his queen and watching his children grow old while he himself stayed young was too much to bear, even though many of them did live unusually long lives. Longevity, in fact, is a trademark of Artur's descendants. By the time he died, many generations of his descendants had already passed before him. It was a terrible burden."

"He died in Wildeor?" asked Sarah.

Tom nodded.

"That accounts for the elaborate tomb we found," said Alex.

Tom fixed his gaze on Alex, frowning. "What of it? The path you were supposed to have taken should have led you clear around the tomb." Tom's frown turned into a scowl, causing Alex to squirm nervously. "So that's how you ended up being chased by the vile creature. You must have taken a wrong turn and disturbed it. Tell me you didn't touch anything in the tomb? Well, did you?"

Alex realized he must have looked as guilty as sin. Sarah nudged him hard in the ribs. "I think you better tell him," she said.

"I . . . only borrowed it."

A troubled expression spread across Tom's face. "Within Artur's tomb were some of the relics I told you about. These are not to be removed! If they wind up in the hands of the Ultima, it would be disastrous. What did you take?"

Alex swallowed hard. "A . . . a sword."

Tom kept his gaze fixed upon Alex. "Where is it now?"

"Downstairs."

For the first time since they'd met, Tom appeared irritated as he demanded Alex retrieve the sword. "And hurry! Let's hope Windlemore knows nothing of this recklessness!"

Alex rushed down the narrow stairs to collect the items in question. Once back in the library, he handed Tom the small sword. Tom took the weapon without saying a word. For many minutes he appeared to study it carefully, scrutinizing every inch of it as if for damage.

Alex was relieved when the old man finally looked up at him and smiled. "You do know what this is, don't you?"

"Yes, sir. It's a short sword."

"This, Alex, is Artur's sword. It is Caldwulf, the sword forged by the Great Power. It has slain many a warrior, many a Keeper, and has been used for both good and evil. It has not left Artur's side since his fight with Ultimus. Indeed, it should be at his side now. I had it embedded in molten rock and placed with his tomb. Yet here it is now, in my hands."

"All I did was pick it up as we passed the tomb," said Alex.

Tom continued to turn the sword over in his hands, as if trying to decide what to do with it. "You really are full of surprises, aren't you?"

To Alex's surprise, the old man passed him the sword. "Well, I suppose it must be yours now, you baffling, puzzling boy. There's so much that even I don't understand. But for you to have simply picked it up, he must have wanted you to have it."

"He who?" asked Sarah.

"Artur, of course. I believe I've told you many times already, there's far more going on in this world than meets the eye. Simply accepting the fact we cannot possibly understand everything that goes on will make things much less complicated and confusing. For example, neither the why or the how of Alex getting this sword matters. What matters is that he has it, and someone wants him to have it. If we're to know why, it will be revealed to us in due course. For now, all we need do is accept the fact. So keep it safe, Alex. It's yours. But under no circumstances let anyone know you have it. Ever. Understood? Especially that confounded Windlemore!"

Tom got up from his chair and headed for the stairway. "I'm off to bed now, and suggest you two do the same. We have much to do, and tomorrow could be a very long day."

Alex had one more question still to ask, and blurted it out before Tom could leave. "You mentioned the first War of Allegiance, Tom, but said nothing of the second."

The old man turned to Alex, a grave expression on his face. "I said nothing because it hasn't happened yet."

CHAPTER 18

A CLOSE CALL

Alex waited patiently for Tom and Sarah to retire before slipping quietly out of the treehouse. The storm had eased, yet despite the rain he planned on paying a second visit to Lake Idlerow. Spurred on by the knowledge that he was the sea dragon's Kindred Spirit, he was eager to see the beast again. Retracing the route taken on his previous visit, his only detour was skirting around the Cracotile shed.

Everything went smoothly until he reached the canal. Portaging around the large gate separating Wid Dewr from Lake Idlerow, he was alarmed by the sound of twigs crackling in the undergrowth nearby. Shining his flashlight about nervously, he saw nothing and so continued on his way. He'd gone no more than a few feet when he again heard the sound of something moving in the bushes, this time even closer.

Unsettled by the thought that he was being followed, Alex jogged briskly along the trail past the gate, worried that whatever was following him now stood between him and the safety of Wid Dewr. Slick and slippery from the rain, the trail had become treacherous, and a sudden misstep saw him tumble into the dense undergrowth. Although his fall was cushioned by the boat-cloak, Alex was devastated to hear the telltale *phssttt* as the vessel deflated. Tearing himself free of the bushes, he dropped the boat and sprang toward the larger lake in a panic.

Rain pelted his face as the storm picked up again, and the rapid flashing of lightning cast eerie shadows around the forest. Glancing over his shoulder, Alex was able to make out the silhouette of something large —and fast—crashing through the undergrowth toward him at breakneck speed.

Outpaced, Alex stopped at the edge of the lake. Turning to face his as-yet-unseen pursuer, he reached for his amulet, but was devastated to find it missing, no doubt lost when he fell. His heart pounding hard as a hammer, he edged backward toward the water knowing full well there was no escape.

Whatever was chasing him was now no more than a few yards away. To Alex's horror, a flash of lightning revealed a deadly Wyvern, one of the most fearsome of the animals included in *The Beasts of Wildeor*. A distant relative of the land dragon, the large winged creature, with its reptilian head, was unpredictable and deadly. Standing twice as tall as a Cracotile on its thick, lizard-legs, the Wyvern bared its teeth as its snake-like head inched closer. Spreading its clawed wings threateningly, the creature craned its long neck skyward and emitted a high-pitched call of victory.

Remembering that he'd brought the sword with him, Alex pulled it from his backpack and pointed it at the Wyvern, hoping some of Artur's magic might save him. The creature looked suspiciously at the weapon for a brief moment, but soon disregarded it as it prepared to wrap its long wings around Alex, its razor sharp claws just inches away, ready to tear him apart. Alex braced for the inevitable.

A sudden commotion in the water distracted the fearsome animal. Alex turned in time to see the massive head of his sea dragon lunge out of the water toward the Wyvern. Outgunned, it turned tail and fled to the safety of the trees.

His heart was still pounding when a gentle nudge from behind caused Alex to turn and face the serpent. He caressed its enormous head. The surge of relief at being rescued was overwhelming, as was the knowledge that the beast somehow seemed to have answered his desperate need for help.

"Thanks, big fella," he said gratefully, stroking the beast's head. As before, the serpent's skin turned translucent as the same bright greens, golds, and reds shimmered to life.

Alex spent the next hour with the sea dragon, only parting ways after it followed him as far as the canal gate. As before, it snorted on him, showering him with serpent snot.

"Will you please cut that out!" said Alex, wiping his face with his sleeve as he walked away. Stopping only long enough to search for his amulet and finding nothing, Alex managed to reinflate the boat-cloak and keep it inflated long enough to get him back to Wid Dewr, all the while wondering how he was going to tell Tom he'd lost the amulet.

* * * * *

"Lost something, have you?" Startled by the unexpected voice from the shadows of the guest room, Alex jumped out of his skin.

He immediately recognized his amulet, swinging like a pendulum as it dangled from Tom's hand. A sardonic smile spread across the old man's face as he stepped into the light. "I thought you were told never to let this out of your sight?" he remarked, passing the amulet to Alex.

Soaking wet and shivering, not to mention extremely embarrassed at having been found out, Alex received the precious jewel thankfully. "Sorry, Tom. It's just . . . well—"

Tom tossed a towel his way. "Enough said, young man. And for heaven's sake, get that serpent mess off you."

Alex nodded numbly. "Why does he keep doing that?"

"He's either allergic to you, cross at you—both highly unlikely, I should add—or he's simply reminding you who you belong to. Territorial beasts, and quite possessive."

"How did you know where I was?"

"It was written all over your face! Such eagerness is nothing new," said Tom, taking a seat on the couch. "You are, after all, your father's son, and an heir of Artur."

Placing the amulet around his neck, Alex asked Tom how he'd found it. Tom clapped his hands and Bogfoot bounded into the room and leapt into the old man's lap. "It was you who taught him to fetch, wasn't it? Anyway, I had him follow you. Some of *The Beasts of Wildeor* are really quite clever, you know."

"Even Dodos?" suggested Alex.

Tom laughed heartily as he stroked the Sasquatch's head. "Except, perhaps, the dotty Dodo. They were a gift, you know, from Mr. Darwin. I'm sure you've heard of him. Delightful chap. He was worried they were a little too friendly for their own good. Interesting ideas about evolution and all that, too. Although he did have a hard time explaining some of the more unusual creatures that call Wildeor home."

Tom motioned for Alex to join him on the couch. "The bond between a Kindred Spirit and his beast is strong. And you, dear boy, have not yet had the benefit of proper training—basic things like how to communicate with your beast. We'll rectify that soon enough, though. At least once we've dealt with Windlemore. Cursed man! I should never have brought him to Wildeor!"

"You brought him here? From where?"

"Found him on my last trip through Africa. He'd been orphaned during the Boer War—terrible affair. I took pity on him and trained him as my apprentice faunician. He eventually worked his way up to warden."

"What's a faunician?"

"They're responsible for the general care and well-being of the animals here, big and small. I suppose we'll be needing another one now. Windlemore was always a little resentful and rebellious. Without my knowing it, he began to delve into the darker side of things after discovering my library. Should never have taught him to read. The rest, as they say, is history."

Tom got up from the couch, a look of apprehension on his face as he began pacing the floor. It was as if something even greater was troubling him. "It's your father," he eventually said gravely.

"Wh . . . what of him?"

"I have reason to believe he may still be alive."

Alex gasped, stunned by the revelation.

Tom pulled a notebook from his pocket, opened it, and handed it to Alex. "I found this amongst Windlemore's papers. It mentions you . . . and your father."

Alex read the section Tom referred to:

ALEX MORTIMER IS NOW IN WILDEOR, THOUGH UNCLEAR HOW HE ESCAPED FROM MORTIMER'S POINT. WE MUST PREPARE HIM FOR ULTIMUS'S RETURN. MAY HE RISE SOON! BOTH MORTIMERS MUST BE MADE APOSTLES OF THE DARKNESS THAT WILL ONCE MORE RULE OVER US . . . OR DIE!

"But . . . but you said my father was already dead," said Alex in disbelief.

"No, I said his body was never found. You assumed he was dead. Granted, that would have been the logical conclusion. But Windlemore's note certainly entertains the possibility that he may still be alive. And I'm unaware of any other Mortimers the Ultima would be interested in."

"He wouldn't join them, would he?" asked Alex.

Tom placed a reassuring hand on Alex's shoulder. "It's possible. I've seen good people, as strong as your father, be turned by Ultimus. It's clear Ultimus hasn't risen yet, and that the Ultima don't even know where he is. But that could change."

"Your father's body was never found," Tom continued. "But that was true of so many men who died in that pointless war. Instinct tells me it is your father that Windlemore speaks of. If so, then we shall find him. And we must do everything in our power to ensure they don't capture you. We've been lucky so far, but we don't have long before Windlemore returns. I suggest we use our time wisely and prepare as best we can. And I, more than anyone, am looking forward to getting my hands on the swine."

"Speaking of swine," said Tom, again switching gears. "I understand you've been introduced to some of my, um, experiments?"

It took Alex a moment to realize what Tom was referring to. "You mean those odd pigs?"

"Odd? I say improved! The Cracotile was one of mine, too."

"Those giant killer chickens?"

Tom smiled sheepishly. "True, true. You're quite right, Alex. I can get a little carried away. I had a lot of time on my hands, you know."

"But is it right? What if the Ultima did it, too . . . mixing up species, breeding terrible monsters?"

"They did once do such things. Terrible, evil creatures."

"Could they do it again?" asked Alex.

"You tell me," said Tom. "You've seen the Ultima."

"Yes . . . now you mention it, they do all look alike."

Tom frowned. "As I feared. They're no doubt messing with man's DNA, too. I never for a moment imagined they'd succeed."

"DNA?" asked Alex, unfamiliar with the term.

"It's what all life consists of," said Tom. "If they've learned how to manipulate it, they can turn men into monsters—soulless, heartless monsters."

Tom sat silent for a few moments before rising to leave the guest room. "The real question is this: will the Ultima ever again produce a monster as horrific as Athoran, the Black Dragon? It's entirely possible. I only hope, for all our sakes, that we can prevent that from ever happening."

CHAPTER 19

UNDER ATTACK

Without warning, the thunderous blast of an explosion echoed across Wildeor, instantly shattering the early morning tranquility. His heart racing, Alex jumped up from the map table in time to see a cascade of water and debris billowing up from the entrance to the underwater tunnel used by Windlemore two days earlier. Where the gate had stood just seconds before—closed by Tom after Windlemore's departure—now only a large gaping hole remained.

Alex rushed to Sarah's side as she trained the telescope in the direction of the explosion. He'd just that minute finished doodling in his notebook, speculating on the Ultima's most likely route into Wildeor:

- WENDIGO CAVE—PROS: DIRECT ROUTE; CONS: WENDIGO EATS PEOPLE.
- OVER THE MOUNTAINS—PROS: NONE; CONS: COLD, IMPENETRABLE FOG, COLD, DANGEROUS, COLD, WOULD TAKE WEEKS. AND COLD.
- FLYING—PROS: DIRECT ROUTE; CONS: TURBULENCE, DIFFICULTY LANDING ON A LAKE FULL OF MONSTERS.
- TUNNEL—PROS: SURPRISE, DIRECT ROUTE; CONS: DANGEROUS,

ONLY POSSIBLE BY SUBMARINE; *ARGONAUT* TOO SMALL TO CARRY ANY ULTIMA.

Only the last option seemed feasible to Alex—it was, after all, how Windlemore travelled to Sawdust City. Which is why he decided they should focus their efforts on the underground passage. Tom, in the meantime, had instructed them to remain in the treehouse's observation deck while he busied himself preparing for Windlemore's return and the impending arrival of the Ultima. What these preparations were he declined to say and Alex forgot to ask—an oversight that now bothered him no end.

"How's that possible?" asked Sarah, stepping aside for Alex. "A huge submarine just came through the tunnel! With a gun on its roof!"

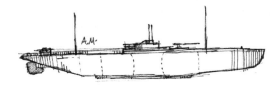

"You mean deck. Submarine's don't have roofs."

"Roof, deck . . . does it really matter?" said Sarah, panic creeping into her voice. "It's big!"

Focusing the telescope on the entrance to the passageway, Alex spotted the sleek black hull of a large submarine as it surfaced. The much smaller *Argonaut* soon appeared behind it, a thick towline connecting them. Alex swivelled the telescope toward Lake Idlerow in search of the sea dragons. If everything Tom said was true, he knew the submarine posed a serious risk to everything in Wildeor.

Alerted by the blast, Tom arrived seconds later looking sprightlier than ever. It was the first time Alex had seen him wearing something other than his pyjamas and smoking jacket. Dressed like an English country gentleman, complete with tweed deerstalker and pipe, he looked like he'd stepped out of the pages of some Victorian novel.

"Very Sherlock," said Sarah.

Tom smiled politely and made straight for the telescope. "Is it them?"

144

Alex swung the telescope back toward the larger submarine in time to see the crew scramble above deck. "I think so. Take a look."

Tom surveyed the scene unfolding below. "Incredible! How did they manoeuvre so large a vessel through those passageways? All those tricky twists and turns."

"Where'd they even get a submarine that big?" asked Alex.

"Probably stole it. Nothing's beneath the Ultima," said Tom as he fiddled with the telescope. "Thought so. It's a U-boat. U-34, it says right there on the conning tower."

"Uh, guys. What's that?" said Sarah pointing toward the eastern end of Lake Idlerow. Squinting into the sun, Alex could see the silhouette of a large, cigar-shaped machine pushing through the clouds above the mountains at the far end of Lake Idlerow. As excited as he was by the appearance of the U-boat—despite the fact it belonged to the Ultima—the completely unexpected arrival of an airship over Wildeor was beyond anything even Alex could have imagined. As big as a battleship, the huge aircraft emerged from the clouds and cruised silently above the lake, casting a massive shadow across the valley as it made its way slowly toward Wid Dewr.

"It's the *Graf Zeppelin*!" said Alex, beyond himself with excitement.

Even Tom was impressed. "It certainly is a thing of beauty. I wonder whose side they're on?"

"Hopefully ours," said Sarah. "Shouldn't we do something, just in case?"

"We will. But first we need to find out who's who and what's what," replied Tom as he again scrutinized the submarines. "Oh dear—"

"Oh dear what?" asked Alex.

"Windlemore's heading toward Lake Idlerow."

"Why would he do that?" asked Sarah. "I thought they were coming for us?"

"Oh, they will. They'll no doubt want to settle a few old scores first."

Sarah was baffled. "What do you mean?"

"During the War of Allegiance, beasts like Alex's were used against the Ultima with great success. They won't have forgotten."

"Can't we stop them?" asked an increasingly concerned Alex.

"They'll come for us first," said Tom. "And remember, they want you alive if possible. That's a good thing."

"Good for who, exactly?" said Sarah.

"You mean good for whom," corrected Tom. "I mean good in the sense that they won't obliterate Wildeor without talking first. Windlemore will have his work cut out finding the books and relics we discussed. He also believes you two are locked up, and that I'm in a coma. That at least gives us a sporting chance."

Sarah frowned at him. "What can the three of us do against a submarine full of blond brutes with guns, and . . . and a balloon full of who-knows-what?"

"Zeppelin," said Alex. "It's a ze—"

"I know!" said an increasingly jumpy Sarah. "And will you both please stop correcting me! It's so annoying."

Tom apologized to Sarah before turning to Alex. "It's not just us and the sea dragons they want. I studied Windlemore's notes last night. They plan on eradicating Wildeor entirely, along with everything in it."

"How?" asked Sarah.

"Brute force," said Tom. "They'll simply chop and burn. But this old man still has a trick or two up his sleeve." Motioning Alex to take over the telescope, Tom made his way to the stairs into the treehouse. "You two stay here until I say otherwise. And keep your heads down!"

Alex did as instructed, watching in silence as the two submarines skirted around Wid Dewr. The crew of the larger vessel cast off the cable connecting them and the smaller *Argonaut* made its way to the landing area closest to the canal. As it docked, Windlemore popped out of the conning tower like a jack-in-the-box. Vaulting ashore, he made his way quickly to the gate separating the moat from Lake Idlerow. After removing a canvas cover from a stash of barrels stacked around the large structure, Windlemore ran back to the *Argonaut*, waving his arms wildly.

"He's signalling them," said Alex. "Wait a minute . . . the gun! They're . . . they're going to blow the gate into Lake Idlerow!"

The roar of the U-boat's deck gun thundered across Wildeor. A split second later, an even louder explosion boomed across the valley as the gunpowder exploded. Alex watched, stunned, as debris flew in every direction like rubble from a volcano. When the smoke cleared, there was no sign of the portcullis.

Alex was beside himself. With the gate gone, the Ultima could now sail unhindered in search of the serpents. "What are we going to do?" he asked, pacing the floor anxiously.

Twisting the ring on her finger nervously, Sarah contemplated the question before responding. "Maybe if I give myself up, they'll leave? They've already got my parents."

"It's me they want, not you! And that damned notebook."

Sarah thumped Alex on the back excitedly. "That's it! The notebook! You've finally had a good idea, Alex Mortimer. If we give those thugs the notebook, with any luck they'll leave us alone."

Alex was mortified at the suggestion. "We can't do that! It contains the secret to Ultimus's resting place," he objected. "Not to mention the fact your parents said we have to keep it safe."

Sarah, however, insisted, and before long she'd managed to convince Alex to at least consider the idea.

"OK, but with one small change," he said. "I'll deliver it!"

Sarah shook her head. "No, you're the Lord of Wildeor, Artur's heir. If they get hold of you, this will all have been for nothing. They'll turn you into one of them, and if they can't, then . . . then—"

"I won't let them take you! This isn't your fight."

Sarah unexpectedly placed her hand against his lips. "We need to stay calm and think this through," she said softly. "Keep an eye on those guys while I find Tom. He'll know what to do."

Relieved that neither he nor Sarah would be put in any immediate danger, Alex turned his attention to the damage around the canal before continuing to scan the shoreline of Lake Idlerow for the sea dragons. After another futile search, he was distracted by the sound of yelling drifting up from the U-boat. He watched transfixed as the black-uniformed crew rushed about busily as they prepared to tie up at the docks. On the far side of the moat, Windlemore was making his way hurriedly to the *Argonaut*, his jacket billowing behind him like a sail as he ran, walking stick in hand.

A droning sound approaching from behind reminded Alex that the zeppelin, too, might yet pose a threat. Zeroing in the airship, he could now clearly see the gondola protruding from its belly. Three powerful engines hung underneath it, while two more attached to its side framed its identification number, *D-LZ127*. Despite the potential threat the huge airship posed—he knew they were used on bombing raids during the Great War—Alex was nevertheless impressed by its enormous bulk as it closed in on him.

The appearance of the zeppelin also caused quite a stir on the docks. The U-boat crew seemed to be in a state of confusion after spotting it, some of them looking skyward and pointing while others busied themselves with the lowering of the gangway before storming ashore. A solitary figure stood on the vessel's tall conning tower, shouting commands as he pointed alternatively at Wid Dewr and the zeppelin. Although the reaction of the crew led Alex to believe the airship was not part of their plan, he still didn't know what it was doing in Wildeor.

What happened next was even more unexpected. As Windlemore docked the *Argonaut* alongside the larger submarine, Alex was stunned to see Sarah led without fuss toward the U-boat by two of the Ultima. Shocked and angry that she'd followed through with her plan to give herself up, Alex raced downstairs in a desperate attempt to get to her before anything bad could happen. Barging into the library, he crashed into Tom, nearly knocking him to the ground.

"Why the blasted rush, Alex?"

"It's Sarah!" said Alex frantically as he helped Tom to his feet. "She's given herself up to the Ultima!"

A troubled expression spread across Tom's face as he reached forward and clasped Alex's shoulders firmly. "You know what she's doing, don't you?"

"She's trying to save her parents!"

"And you! But if she thinks they'll take her to her parents by giving up the notebook, she's much mistaken."

Alex was frantic. "We have to do something, Tom. Before it's too late!"

"Help is on its way, trust me. And soon."

Alex struggled to free himself from Tom's grasp, but the old man was stronger than he looked and was clearly determined to prevent Alex from acting brashly. "Sacrifices sometimes need to be made," said

Tom. "Sarah seems prepared to make such a sacrifice to save her parents. But you must trust me when I tell you no harm will come to her. It's not her time."

Despite Tom's reassurances, Alex couldn't resist the overwhelming urge to help his friend. They'd been through too much together to abandon her now. Twisting free of Tom, he bolted for the stairs.

Alex raced toward the aerial tramway only to find the platform empty. With no choice but to take the route he used to visit his sea dragon, he climbed quickly down the tree before charging recklessly along the rope bridge. As he bounced along the unstable connection between Wid Dewr and the docks, he heard a familiar whine behind him and turned around in time to see Bogfoot chasing after him. Worried the animal might come to harm, he tried to shoo the Sasquatch away. But the small creature ignored him, and continued following him as he completed the crossing.

Once clear of the buildings, Alex had an uninterrupted view of the activity on the docks. Sarah had been hauled aboard the U-boat and was being questioned by Windlemore. Bursting onto the dock and brandishing the small handgun he'd picked up in the Wendigo's cave, the small element of surprise he'd achieved vanished as the Ultima realized he was alone—and just a boy. Despite dodging and weaving his way past the first few crew members, he was soon tackled and forced to drop his weapon.

"Let her go, Windlemore!" he shouted. "I've got the notebook! I know where the sword is, too! Let her go and I'll tell you everything!"

Alex heard Windlemore shouting in an unfamiliar language as the crewmen lugged him along the dock and dumped him at the officer's feet. The man's jet-black uniform was crumpled and grimy, and he smelt like oil and smoke. To Alex's dismay, the sleeves of his jacket bore a skull and crossbones insignia. As fearsome as the intimidating man who wore it, the motif was similar to the one Alex had seen in the Greystone notebook. It had fire engulfing the skull, and its mouth was locked in a sinister grin. This same insignia had apparently been carved into the flesh of one of his ancestors—Graham Mortimer.

With skin weathered like old leather, the officer's unkempt pepper-black hair protruded from his sailor's cap and his scraggly beard was speckled with spit and crumbs. He was, Alex quickly learned, not a man to mess with.

Picking up Alex's pistol, the officer inspected the weapon's chamber, smirking when he found it empty. He barked a command, and a crewman quickly loaded the pistol and handed it back to the superior officer who tucked it into his belt.

"I'll keep this, seeing as you're not man enough to use it," he said in a thick Eastern European accent. He then seized Alex roughly by the throat, his calloused, nicotine-stained hand squeezing so hard Alex could scarcely breathe. Just as it seemed he was about to pass out, the officer let go.

Falling to his knees and gasping as his lungs filled with air, Alex took a few moments to gather enough strength to face the officer. "Tell Windlemore to let her go!" he said hoarsely.

The big man placed his hands on his hips, threw back his head and let out a whoop of laughter. Turning to Windlemore, he shouted: "Hear that, Warden? The boy says you have to let her go!"

Windlemore laughed. "Play nice, Tier. And don't hurt him! At least not yet. If you want to hurt someone, save it for the girl."

Alex watched as Sarah's captors tore off her backpack. As she struggled to get it back, he was horrified to see Windlemore strike her hard enough across the face that she crumpled to the ground. "Keep your filthy hands off her!" he shouted.

Fiery contempt burning in his eyes, Windlemore jumped onto the docks and strode toward Alex, stopping only when he stood between the boy and Tier. "Shut up, Mortimer!" he spat venomously. "You've been nothing but trouble since the moment I set eyes on you."

Windlemore grabbed Alex's face, squeezing hard and sneering in pleasure at the boy's discomfort. "Yes, Mortimer, it is you we want. And believe me, you'll curse this day for the rest of your life!"

Alex spat at Windlemore, upsetting the scrawny little man so much that he drew his walking stick up high and struck him hard across the face, drawing blood. Alex dropped to the ground, dazed by the severity of the blow. Looking up indignantly, he watched in silence as Windlemore wiped the phlegm from his face.

"Don't you ever try anything like that again, Mortimer! You've no idea what we're capable of."

Despite the intense pain raging through his head, Alex did his best to give Windlemore his most defiant look. "How could you betray Wildeor?"

Windlemore smirked. "Let's just say I was born nasty."

Windlemore instructed Tier to take Alex aboard the submarine. "We've got much to do if we're to find what we're looking for and wipe this place off the map. Lock him up, and use whatever force is needed to find out what he knows!"

Tier smiled menacingly as he ordered Alex to be taken aboard the submarine. "What about the girl?"

"Let me find out what she knows. You can have what's left."

Opening Sarah's backpack, Windlemore yelled furiously when all he found were rocks. Striding back to the submarine, the warden was furious at Sarah's trick. Hauling her to her feet roughly by the hair, he pressed his face close to hers. Alex watched helplessly as Windlemore pulled a small dagger from his coat and held it against her throat.

"Where's that little book you promised me?" Windlemore shouted menacingly, still clasping her hair. "Could it be in here?" he said, reaching toward her baggy shirt. Sarah instinctively tried to pull herself free from Windlemore's clawing hands. He laughed ominously. "Gutsy, aren't you? I like girls with spirit."

Alex felt hopeless as Windlemore tormented Sarah. "Leave her alone! She's done nothing!" he hollered.

Before he could say anything more, Tier punched him hard in the stomach. "At least the girl's got guts, not like you, Mortimer."

As Alex fell to the ground, a commotion erupted on the dock just a few feet away. To his dismay he heard Bogfoot yelp after being kicked aside by one of the Ultima. Horrified, he saw Tier aim his gun at the defenceless creature now cowering at the edge of the dock. Before Tier could pull the trigger, Alex kicked at him, ruining his aim. Instead of hitting the Sasquatch, the bullet struck one of the submarine crew in the arm.

The relief he felt as Bogfoot escaped was short-lived. Without warning, the officer turned and pistol-whipped him across the face, knocking him to the deck. "Get him aboard!" he growled. Barely conscious, Alex felt himself being dragged along the dock toward the submarine. His head throbbed from the blow, his jaw felt as if it was broken as blood trickled from his lips.

"Lock him in the hold," said Tier. "We'll deal with him once we get this place burning!"

Despite the pain coursing through his body, Alex became aware of a comforting presence nearby. It was the same feeling he had whenever he was near his sea dragon. This time, however, it was a reassuring sense that help was on its way. He was right. Alerted by the shouts of the crew, he looked up to see his sea dragon, the undisputed Beast of Wildeor, rising steadily out of the water beside the submarine. The sudden appearance of the huge creature had the Ultima crew scrambling in all directions.

Only Tier seemed to keep his cool. "Man your stations!" he hollered. "Have you never seen a sea monster before?" He had to shoot one of the hysterical deckhands before he was able to get the attention of his panicked crew. "Open fire, all weapons!" he bellowed.

The moment the beast appeared, the Ultima dropped Alex, who then managed to crawl toward a stack of crates piled on the dock. Although drifting in and out of consciousness as the action unfurled around him, he did witness Sarah lunging at Windlemore. Grabbing hold of his amulet, she yanked it off his neck with a sharp tug. Sensing Windlemore's vulnerability, the sea dragon snatched the scraggy man in his massive jaws. Shaking its prey vigorously from side to side the way a cat would a mouse, the beast tossed Windlemore onto the shore where he lay wounded, barely able to move. The sea dragon then lowered its head toward the submarine as the crew fled in all directions. It surveyed the crew, selecting its next target, prioritizing those who posed the greatest threat. Alex was relieved when it made short work of the gun crew.

As the skirmish continued, the shouting and gunfire around the dock was joined by a familiar squawking sound coming from the buildings along the shore. Alex saw at least a dozen Cracotiles descend upon a group of armed Ultima who had become separated from their submarine. The giant birds took a heavy toll on the crew, even though the men had weapons. Windlemore, defenceless without his protective amulet, and severely injured, screamed horribly as he disappeared in a flurry of beaks and talons.

As the remaining Ultima crew escaped below deck, Alex heard Tier shout an order to a crew member close to him. "Get the boy up here, quickly."

The crewman made it to within a few feet of Alex when the huge sea dragon struck, clamping its mighty jaws upon the man, dealing with him just as it had done with Windlemore. But before the sea dragon could do anything more to help, Tier raised his pistol, pointing it directly at Alex.

"If we can't have you, Mortimer, nobody will!" he shouted as he squeezed the trigger.

The tremendous agony Alex felt in his stomach as the bullet pierced his soft flesh was beyond anything he'd yet experienced. Miraculously, the searing hot pain subsided almost immediately into a numbness as he drifted toward unconsciousness. Clutching his hand to his stomach, Alex instinctively tried to stem the heavy flow of blood oozing from the wound. Just before losing all awareness, he glanced upward at the submarine in time to see Tier fire the gun at him a second time.

Pushed backward onto the dock from the force of the gunshot to his chest, the last thing Alex saw was the huge airship floating into view above him.

CHAPTER 20

THE LIGHT THAT NEVER GOES OUT

Alex's life didn't flash before him. Nor did he find a stairway leading toward some beckoning bright light. In fact, if asked to describe his out-of-body experience, he'd have said it was like watching a movie in slow motion—very slow motion—as the real world around him advanced almost imperceptibly one frame at a time.

He felt as if he was floating, and was surprised to feel no sorrow or fear as he gazed down upon his bloodied and battered body. Instead, he felt an inexplicable sense of release, of freedom, of peace. Gone was the intense pain caused by the bullets and the beating. Gone, too, was the anger and hatred he'd felt toward his assailants.

He felt as weightless as a cloud. Free of the confusion that had erupted upon the dock, he drifted effortlessly toward Sarah, frozen in mid-stride as she ran toward his earthly body, one arm outstretched, the other clutching Windlemore's amulet, her expression a mix of shock and horror.

The Beast of Wildeor—his beast—also stared in his direction. But unlike the humans around him, the beast saw Alex as he now was, not the motionless body dying on the dock. It knew exactly where he was. The Ultima crew cowered in fear at the ferocity of the unexpected attack, their faces locked in expressions of terror. With the arrival of the sea dragon, their attack had clearly been thwarted, although it was evident they were hell-bent on causing as much destruction as possible.

It was then that Alex noticed the shadows. Not the dark shadows cast by the humans around him, but the barely visible traces of white, almost translucent, light that shimmered gently as they darted about the scene. At the same time, he became aware of the faint whispering of soft, soothing voices. It seemed as if two worlds coexisted side by side—the physical world with its pain, sorrow, and hatred; and this unfamiliar, otherworldly place of light and delicate white shadows.

Time meant nothing in this unfamiliar in-between place. There was no night, no day, no hunger, no thirst, no past, no present—just the constant, comforting glow that enveloped him like a parent's soothing touch. There was no reason to fear anything in this strange yet safe place. And he liked it.

Alex became aware of a group of these formless beings gravitating toward him, circling momentarily before darting off as quickly and silently as hummingbirds. As they became more confident, they began to brush against him, causing him to tingle with delight.

The white shadows were gliding about so closely, he could touch them, his hand passing right through them. It was then he became aware of another, larger white shadow moving toward him.

"Who are you?" he asked.

The reply came from a voice as soft as velvet, one he sensed rather than heard. "We are you, Alex. As you once were, as you will be again."

Alex was confused. "Am I dead?"

"There is no death. Only being, or not being. Only light, or dark."

"Then, where am I?" he asked.

"Where do you want to be?"

"Here! Can I stay here with you?"

The swirling shadow of light took on an almost human form, pulsing gently as it moved around him. "Do I know you?" he asked.

For a fleeting moment, Alex thought he could see the semblance of a woman's face in the swirling vapour, gentle and full of love and compassion. "It is best that you return, Alex," it said gently. "You have so much left to do. There are some who want you to return to them."

"Who? I have no family, no friends."

"Yes you do, Alex. For the first time you have been living the life intended for you. There will be much pain to endure, much suffering, but the sacrifices will ultimately be worth it."

"But I don't want to go back! It hurts so much. There's so much sadness."

"You have nothing to fear, Alex. Although you won't see us, we will always be with you." Alex watched the shadow slowly fade to grey and then to nothingness as the voice repeated the words, "You have nothing to fear."

"Wait! Who are you? Come back!"

An intense throbbing in his chest caused Alex to double up in agony as he felt himself falling, falling, falling.

CHAPTER 21

A WARM WILDEORIAN WELCOME

"Alex? Can you hear me?" The voice, though muffled, sounded strangely familiar. "Welcome back! You made it!"

Blinking as his eyes adjusted to the light, Alex at first failed to recognize his surroundings, or the middle-aged man standing beside his bed. After a few moments, however, he realized he was in the room where he'd first set eyes on the old man who lived in a tree. But the man standing before him looked a little less familiar.

"You don't remember me?"

Alex stared at him blankly. Then it clicked. "Tom? But . . . but you look so much younger."

Tom smiled kindly at Alex. Gone were the deep creases that had lined his face; he'd gained weight and muscle tone, and exuded an energy and vitality that Alex hadn't seen before.

"Why do I hurt so much?" he asked weakly as he tried to sit up.

Tom placed a cushion behind his head to prop him up. "You've been gone a long time."

"How long, exactly?"

"Almost two months. It's a miracle you're still with us. It was touch and go for a while."

Alex tried to recall what had led to his current state. "The Ultima . . . what happened?"

"After you left me in Wid Dewr and ran to the docks, I knew we were in trouble. My first thought was to revisit my earlier incarnation as the stone giant. Remember that?"

Alex nodded. "Did it work?"

Tom smiled. "Sadly, no. Soul shifting requires tremendous effort and energy, and after that earlier encounter with the Ultima, not to mention the Wendigo, I had nothing more to give on that front. I knew our only hope was your sea dragon, and of course the Cracotiles."

"Where was he? I remember looking for him, with the telescope."

"They nest at the far end of Lake Idlerow."

Alex looked surprised. "I didn't know they nested."

"You have much to learn about *The Beasts of Wildeor*, Alex. Sea dragons are very reclusive creatures and will nest underwater, usually where there's a cave that's well hidden. It's an instinct they developed hiding from the Ultima. I had my work cut out calming him, he was so anxious to get to you."

"You can communicate with them?" asked Alex.

"Can't you?" Tom said with a wry grin. "Something else we'll have to work on. After disposing of Windlemore so effortlessly—such a fitting end to such a despicable a man—your sea dragon set upon the crew. Along with the Cracotiles, they made short work of those Ultima that weren't able to make it back to the submarine. More than twenty, all told, buried now by the lake. All blond. They looked like brothers."

"I do remember," said Alex. He pulled back his pyjama top and inspected a small scar marking the impact point of the first bullet. He was surprised, however, to find only a faint bruise near his heart where the second bullet struck him.

"He shot me twice. Tier, I think it was. But there's no scar. What happened?"

Tom reached into his jacket pocket. "This happened," he said, dropping what was left of Alex's pocket watch onto his lap. "You could say your father saved your life."

The face of the watch was entirely smashed in, the metal casing dented by the impact of the bullet. It looked as if someone had taken a hammer to it.

"The first bullet caused the most damage," said Tom. "Got you in the stomach, but luckily hit nothing vital. The second hit you in the chest, right in the heart. Fortunately for all of us, that's where you carried your watch. Here, I thought you might want to keep this, too, as a souvenir." Tom handed Alex the short-barrelled British Bulldog pistol he'd been shot with. "Took out the bullets, though."

Alex placed the gun on the table beside him, barely able to conceal his distaste for the weapon. "I saw the zeppelin. And... and parachutes, I think. Were they on our side?"

Tom smiled. "Yes, they were on our side. Typical of young Lonsdale—or Lonnie, or Mop, or whatever else you call him—to make so dramatic an entrance, and from such a spectacular aircraft. He's one well-connected fellow, that's for sure."

"What about the cloud cover?" asked Alex.

"I asked the very same thing," said Tom. "Apparently it wasn't a problem so long as they flew very, very slowly. Anyway, he and a dozen or so of his aviator friends landed in time to see off the submarine. Well, all except for one. He ended up stuck high up in the branches of Wid Dewr for a few hours before anyone noticed. Wasn't until he started playing his bagpipes that we found him!"

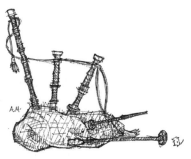

"Funny, I thought I heard bagpipes in my dreams."

"Did some wee Sasquatch say bagpipes?" boomed a voice from the stairwell. Alex was left speechless as the large, familiar frame of Red McPhee burst into the room. Equally as surprising, he was cradling Bogfoot in his arms like a baby. If Alex didn't know better, he would have sworn the tiny animal looked as if it was smiling. "Tom hollered down to me that you were wakin', lad! I'm so glad to see you up! It's a miracle, state you were in."

The big man grinned widely as he approached Alex and grabbed his hand. The transformation in the stoker was almost as dramatic as that of Tom. Gone were the ever-present coal-covered overalls, now replaced by a clean—for Red McPhee—pair of denim dungarees and a plaid shirt.

"Aye, laddie, it's me alright," he said. "You're wee pilot pal came and fetched me. Promised me a ride in that great big balloon. Didn't need much persuading. You know, a friend in need and all that. Not to mention a tree with hot and cold running water! Who'd have thought it? That, and the new job—"

"What job?" Alex asked, confused.

It was Tom who filled Alex in regarding the details of Red McPhee's new position. "Well, seeing as our last warden was eaten by some of the creatures under his care, we thought we'd ask your friend Algeo here if he'd like the job. He does like animals, as you were so careful to point out to us."

Alex laughed aloud. "Sorry, did you say Algeo?"

"Aye, lad," said Red McPhee. "After all your heckling, I decided I probably should have a proper name after all."

"I was only joking," said Alex. "Algeo's hardly a proper name, is it?"

Red McPhee smiled. "Aye. But your friend Tom here seems to like it. But then again, nice bloke and all, he is a bit old-fashioned."

Tom chuckled. "Looks like I'll have my work cut out with you two!"

Red McPhee placed a hand on Alex's shoulder. "I best be off now, lad. A lot of strange wee beasties need looking after. Rest up, and we'll soon have you out and about doing the rounds with me."

Seeing his old stoker friend reminded Alex there were other friends still unaccounted for. "Where's Sarah?" he asked.

"She's doing just fine," said Tom reassuringly. "Once the Ultima left, the *Graf Zeppelin* was able to land safely. It couldn't stay long. As you'll recall it was about to begin its first around-the-world voyage. So Lonsdale accompanied Sarah back to New York aboard the airship. Although she couldn't wait to leave Wildeor, she was devastated not to be able to return to school. Far too dangerous. Like you, she has to keep a low profile until everything blows over. If it ever does blow over."

Tom's face brightened as if he suddenly remembered something of importance. "Did I mention that Sarah's now a Kindred Spirit?"

Alex shook his head.

"Well, seems the smaller sea dragon took quite a liking to her. It was a sight to behold, and quite unexpected. Especially for Sarah."

Alex smiled broadly at the thought of Sarah and the smaller sea dragon. "What about the notebook? Did they get away with it?"

"It's safe. It's here in Wildeor. Clever girl, that Sarah."

"What about her parents? Can you help them?"

"Yes, I believe we can," said Tom. "Lonsdale's on his way there as we speak. He stayed aboard the airship to Europe, so should be in Addis Ababa by now to see what he can find out about the Greystones. Oh, that reminds me—they each left something for you. I stashed everything away until you were well enough to receive them."

Alex watched with keen interest as Tom reached under the bed and pulled out an old suitcase. "You obviously made quite an impression. They both insisted on leaving something special for you."

To Alex's astonishment, Tom pulled out Mop's flying jacket. It was the same one the flying ace wore when attacked by the Red Baron. "He told me to tell you he's going to teach you to fly, too. Says you're a natural."

He then handed Alex a small envelope. "And this is from Sarah. It was all she had left after you apparently helped lose all her luggage. She was adamant you have it."

Alex tore open the envelope to find Sarah's gold ring, the one she played with constantly whenever nervous or unhappy. "Her parents gave it to her, but she wanted you to have it." Alex tried to place the ring on his middle finger, but it was too small, so he slipped it onto the pinky of the same hand he wore his mother's ring on. It was a tight fit, and he knew he'd have a heck of a time taking it off if she ever wanted it back. Which, he hoped, would never happen.

"Oh yes!" said Tom excitedly as he suddenly remembered something more. "Back in a jiffy."

Tom returned minutes later clutching the Wid Dewr guest book. Alex read the newest entry with surprise. "Colonel Walden was here?"

"He was travelling across the continent when he heard from Lonsdale that the new Lord of Wildeor—that would be you, naturally—had at last arrived. He was adamant on paying a visit. Very adventurous sort, too. He arrived with the rescue team that parachuted out of the zeppelin. Remarkable man. When the time comes, I know he'll be an important ally."

Tom pulled from his jacket yet another gift. It was a pocket watch almost identical to his. "When Colonel Walden heard that the watch he'd given your father was smashed, he insisted on giving you this."

Engraved on the back of the silver casing were the words: ONE OF THE FEW. FRIENDS ALWAYS, MORTY. Opening the case eagerly, Alex was thrilled to find the same intricately designed W as was engraved in his watch. This time the engraved text read DOMNE LIGEANTIA.

"It's Latin for Lord of Allegiance," said Tom. "He said your father gave it to him."

"Will I ever meet Colonel Walden, to thank him?"

"I believe so. But he's got some work of his own to do before joining us on the adventure that lies ahead."

"Adventure? Talk about putting a positive spin on things!"

Tom smiled. "For now, our priorities must be to find the Greystones and rebuild the Allegiance. You, Alex, will play a vital role in rebuilding the Allegiance before it's too late."

Alex slumped back into his bed, suddenly tired. "What use can I be? I'm nothing, a nobody. I couldn't even stop the Ultima from taking Sarah! Can't I just stay here and help Red look after the animals?"

"For now, yes. But you must learn the ways of the Allegiance and how to harness the gifts you've been given. If, that is, you want to help.

The choice is yours, Alex. Despite your importance, you cannot be forced to help. It is a choice that must be made of your own free will."

Tom got up to leave. "But enough for now! This has been too much excitement for one day. You need rest or we'll never have you back to normal. If, as Sarah would say, you ever were normal."

Alex smiled as he lay down to rest. "You're a fine one to talk. How many people do you know that live in a tree?"

"Good point," replied Tom. "Just you, me, and Red McPhee, I suppose."

Chapter 22

BIG DECISIONS

Time in Wildeor didn't follow the usual rules. It seemed to pass by ever so slowly as the minutes trudged their way to hours, the hours dragged themselves into days, and the days wandered aimlessly toward weeks. The slow, but sure, pace of his recovery suited him well after the unexpected excitement and adventure he'd faced that remarkable summer of 1929.

Now, as the cooler air of autumn arrived with its colour and promise of peace, he was strong enough to assist Red McPhee in his new duties as Warden of Wildeor. He enjoyed designing and building the new gates for use between the moat and Lake Idlerow, as well as the one needed to protect the tunnel entrance into Wildeor. He even helped Tom complete Mop's defogging machine, which meant in future the aviator would be able to fly directly into Wildeor—so long as they knew he was coming and remembered to turn it on. He learned a great deal more about the diverse animal and plant life this spectacular hidden sanctuary hosted. Above all else, he was thrilled to have found his real home.

But his greatest pleasure was undoubtedly spending time with his sea dragon. The bonding was a crucial part of their mutual growth and development, and Alex came to spend a good portion of each day in the company of the magnificent creature—his Beast of Wildeor—as Tom instructed him in the care of a serpent.

Alex had changed in other ways, too. His near-death experience, which he thought about often, gave him new confidence. The encouraging prophecy he'd been given—that he had nothing to fear—became his guiding principle, and helped him overcome the most difficult tasks assigned to him.

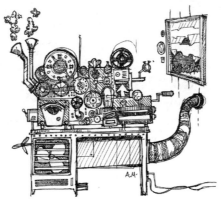

Mop's De-fogging Machine

Which is why, when Tom asked if he was ready to accept his role as a member of the Allegiance, he was confused by his inability to say yes. He and Tom had travelled to the far end of Lake Idlerow aboard the repaired boat-cloak. Tom, like Sarah before him, had doubted the odd little vessel's seaworthiness, and Alex relished the opportunity to prove its capabilities.

Climbing to the ledge where he and Sarah had last seen the Wendigo, they checked that the rocks keeping the evil creature confined to his cave were still in place. Tom then led Alex to a concealed entrance a few feet away.

"This is where you should have exited," said Tom. "If, of course, you had done as Mop told you and stuck to the trail. Still, doing what you're told has always been an issue for you Mortimers."

Turning their back on the entrance, they sat down and rested, enjoying the same amazing view Alex had last seen when arriving in Wildeor.

It was Tom who eventually broke the silence. Leaning forward, he rested his chin on the walking stick he'd taken to carrying around with him. "Have you ever wondered what your name means?"

"It means strong. I looked it up."

"Yes, it does indeed mean strong. Despite what you think, it is an appropriate name for you. Being strong doesn't just mean being able to lift boulders or carry mighty weapons. It applies equally to strength of character and resolve. You score highly in both areas. Much more so than you give yourself credit for. But what I meant was the name Mortimer."

Alex shook his head.

"The Mortimer name came about after the War of Allegiance. It actually means dead water. It was a cover-up to protect Artur and his descendants. I remember it like it was yesterday. When the fighting ended, the bodies of the slain—man and beast—were cast into the sea. Artur oversaw the gruesome task himself. The locals took to calling their hero Lord Morte du Mer—Lord of the Dead Sea, a name that followed him as he moved amongst the Chieftains. Over the years it was simplified to Mortimer, a name that Artur and his heirs came to prefer in order to hide their true lineage."

From their vantage point high above Lake Idlerow, Alex could see the two sea dragons cavorting in the distance, leaping high out of the water, then diving out of sight. Seconds later they would reappear further up the long lake, causing waves large enough to tip a boat.

Tom smiled wistfully at the sight.

"Did you ever have a beast of your own?" Alex asked.

"I did," said Tom with a tinge of sadness. "Remarkable creature. There's never been anything quite like it since."

Alex sensed Tom's anguish. "Was it the Red Dragon? Iddraig?"

Tom nodded, and silence once more enveloped them as each was lost in their thoughts.

It was Tom who eventually spoke. "There's no place more beautiful than this anywhere in the world."

"You should know," said Alex. "You've been just about everywhere, seen just about everything."

"So true. As I think I may already have mentioned, I had—"

"A lot of time on my hands!" said Alex, finishing the sentence for Tom.

They both laughed. "Not so sure if it's true anymore," continued Tom. "Winter's coming and already I'm hearing reports of unrest around the world. It's no doubt fuelled by the Ultima, and aimed at stirring up hatred amongst men, to win them over to their side before they try once more to sink this curious little planet into darkness."

"What's been happening?" asked Alex.

"The world's money markets have collapsed," said Tom. "The Wall Street Crash, they're calling it. It looks as if it will bankrupt a great many countries. And bankrupt countries mean the rise of dictatorships. It's already started in Europe. Others will follow. When that happens, all hell will break loose. Especially if Ultimus is resurrected and spreads his influence amongst them."

Tom paused for quite some time, leaving Alex to ponder the gravity of what he had said. When he did finally speak, Alex was somewhat taken aback by his directness. "We all face choices at some point in our lives. It's your turn now, Alex."

"What do you mean?"

Tom placed a hand on Alex's shoulder. "If you join the Allegiance, then there's a chance we will win. It will, of course, be dangerous and difficult. If you choose not to fulfil your destiny, then there is no chance of victory. No doubt you'd have some peace and quiet here in Wildeor for a short while. Years, perhaps. Then . . . well, the world will once again become a terrible place. If you only ever heed one piece of advice I give you, Alex, you might want to make it this: it is better to go through life regretting the things you did do, rather than the things you didn't do."

As Tom's words sank in, he handed Alex the walking stick he'd been leaning on. It was the very same one he'd used to unlock the door the day he and Sarah rescued Tom. "Take it. It's yours now. Heaven knows you deserve it."

Alex was puzzled. "Won't you need it to get in and out of Wid Dewr? At least your part of it?"

Tom chuckled. "These things are much more than just keys. You'll find out soon enough. And anyway, I can't think of any reason why I'd want to lock you out. Or in, for that matter. Unless, of course, you insist on bringing more animals in."

"It's only Bogfoot."

"It wasn't your Sasquatch I was referring to," said Tom. "You mean you've forgotten about your egg?"

"The Cracotile!" exclaimed Alex.

"Unless you're ready for parenthood, I suggest you put it back where you found it. There's still time."

Alex remained quiet as he surveyed the scene below. The trees around the lake were rapidly changing colour with the onset of autumn, and he could see the magnificent tones spread beneath them like some huge canvas—the rich reds and yellows of the vast maples and oaks, here and there interspersed with the dark green of the conifers—the same colours, he noted, that his sea dragon turned whenever he touched it. In the distance, he could make out the giant golden oak in all its glory, healthy again thanks to Sarah's quick thinking.

"What will it be, Alex?" said Tom. "Will you let me train you in the ways of the Allegiance? Will you fulfil your destiny?"

"I . . . I don't know. It's just . . . well, it's so much responsibility. I'm not sure I'm ready for it . . . if I'll ever be ready for it."

Tom stretched out on the ground beside him. "I understand. But time is running out. Precisely how much time we have I can't say. It's not we who hold the cards. They do. And while our little run-in with them here in Wildeor no doubt set them back, they'll soon recover and will be back, stronger and better organized. We need to take the fight to them. All I ask is that you don't wait too long."

Alex considered the older man's words carefully. Try as he might, he still couldn't be sure that he, an orphan from Mortimer's Point, had what it would take to fill the shoes of a hero like Artur.

"Stop thinking so hard!" said Tom, sensing his predicament. "It's giving me a headache just watching you. The right answer will present itself soon enough, trust me."

"How . . . how will I know what the right answer is? I'm just so confused."

"You just answered that question yourself. A right answer never comes swaddled in confusion or fear. You'll just know. Simple as that. You have nothing to fear."

Alex looked at Tom, surprised to hear him utter the same phrase he'd heard from the white shadows. But seeing that Tom was paying him no attention, he considered his use of the phrase a coincidence.

"You're right," said Alex eventually, flopping onto the grass. "I won't sweat it. It'll come to me."

"That a boy," said Tom. "Tomorrow's another day!"

"Can I ask a favour, Tom?"

"Fire away, my boy. Anything at all."

"Promise me no more giant man-eating chickens?"

Tom laughed long and hard. "I do so love dabbling in nature! But if you insist. Anyway, I suppose I'll be far too busy teaching you how to be a proper Lord of Wildeor."

"Do you really think I can do it?"

"Yes, Alex, I do. I'm convinced you'll prove a worthy successor to your father. And a winter here in Wildeor is just the thing you need to cure you of any doubts you might have concerning your abilities. It may help you to know that Artur felt much the same way at first. And look how much he achieved."

Alex sighed deeply. "Yes, but I'm no Artur."

"Oh, but you will be," said Tom confidently. "And probably a lot sooner than you think."

The End

Every book owes its existence to a host of characters, real and imagined. I'd like to extend a huge and heartfelt "Thank you" to the following very wonderful (and real) folks for their encouragement during the writing and editing of Alex Mortimer & The Beast of Wildeor:

Kim, Cameron and Caleb (for putting up with me during the 30,660 hours that passed from start to finish);
Mum/Nana/Sylvia (three great women all rolled into one);
The Godard family (Richard, Jackie, Shaun, Adam and Nick);
The Orvis family (Nathan, Leona and Tom Dearsley);
The Other Dearsley family (Graham, Lucy, Leah and Joel);
Brenda Patterson (for believing in the vision);
Les and Marijane Dakens (for their kindness and encouragement);
Uwe, Monika, Evelyn and Kurt Wolff (for all the coffee and fact checking);
The McPhee family (Andrew, Joyce and Eilish);
Kevan Anne Murray (for learning to draw like a 14 year-old boy);
Susan Pryke (for her wonderful editing, and for getting me started as a writer all those years ago);
John "F" Mather (for his support in the transportation department);
Maryleah otto (for her continuing encouragement);
Dr. R. Gupta (for his medical skills);
My old school chums Nic, Jonathan and Toby (for staying friends despite the years);
And finally, Garry Mortimer (for the informal history lesson regarding the Mortimer name).

B.A. Dearsley is an odd mix of the Old and the New Worlds. Born in Canada and raised in England, he's a graduate of the second oldest school in Britain (King's School Rochester, founded in 604 AD) as well as Stirling University in Scotland where his love of history, haggis and Hogmanay deepened. After twenty years as an editor and writer, he's now writing novels full-time.

COMING SOON: BOOK 2 IN THE
"ALEX MORTIMER" SERIES

ALEX MORTIMER & THE LORDS
OF ALLEGIANCE

VISIT
WWW.THEBEASTOFWILDEOR.COM
FOR DETAILS